AMERICAN STANDARD

DRUE HEINZ LITERATURE PRIZE 2002

AMERICAN STANDARD

JOHN BLAIR

UNIVERSITY OF PITTSBURGH PRESS

For Sandy and James

Published by the University of Pittsburgh Press, Pittsburgh, Pa., 15260

Copyright © 2002, John Blair

All rights reserved

Manufactured in the United States of America

Printed on acid-free paper

10 9 8 7 6 5 4 3 2 1

ISBN 0-8229-4192-9

The terror is, all promises are kept.
Even happiness.

Robert Penn Warren, "Treasure Hunt"

Bathrooms Made for the Soul

**Slogan for the American Standard Company's line
of vitreous china bathroom fixtures**

CONTENTS

★

AMERICAN STANDARD

BACON ON THE BEACH

★ ★ ★

He walks gingerly out into the water, feeling for broken glass. Mud squeezes up cool between his toes. When the water is chest deep, he pushes up from the bottom muck out into the lake. He aims for a yellow porch light on the far shore and starts swimming, plowing through the chilly water in a slow freestyle.

Halfway across, he turns over onto his back, breathing hard against the cottony wetness of the air. He feels tight all over but not crampy.

This late, all he can see of his neighbors is the occasional flash of a car's headlights as someone pulls into a driveway or the bitter blue flicker of a television, far off, framed in a window.

Winter is short in this part of Florida, though the March air is still crisp sometimes at night. The chill keeps people inside, which is good. Only once, as far as he knows, has anyone noticed him out in the water. He had made it to the far shore and turned back when he heard voices in the dark. Two people, a man and a woman, had stood up from the matted Bermuda grass of the lawn and peered through the darkness at him.

"Nutria, or big damn catfish," a man's voice had said, very distinct in the clear night air.

He was a mystery to them then, disconnected and maybe a little frightening. It was a great sensation.

Tonight he stops thirty yards out from the far shore of the lake and treads water. Somewhere beyond the first row of houses, the ones on the lake, someone turns up headbanger music loud enough that he can feel its beat inside the water around him. It plays that way for twenty or thirty seconds, then it's turned suddenly back down. He can hear voices, then the flat, high sound of laughter echoing across the water.

Kids. Some of the college students who rent the duplexes farther back from the lake. The development is only a mile or so from the university. When he had first moved in, he'd resented them and their music and the way they roared down the streets in their daddies' BMWs, running down dogs and making pests of themselves. Now, somehow, the frantic sound of their music seems comfortable.

He takes a deep breath, letting the air buoy him up so that he floats on his back. When he exhales the rusty smell of the water through his nose he has to flutter his arms a bit to keep his chest and face above water. The water is just warm enough that a thin, smoky haze rises from it into the cooler night air.

He floats that way for a long time, listening for the occasional sound from the faraway world of the human. Cats yowl somewhere, mating. He feels detached and serene.

When he finally eases back over and starts to swim slowly toward his own porch light, the moon has begun to rise, almost full, ponderous and flat on the horizon beyond the roofs. He feels enormously comfortable, and he has to fight the urge to roll back over and lie face up on the water and just drift until he falls asleep.

★

Three weeks before she left, his wife had suddenly decided that his son needed a dog. Jack thinks about this, wading through the last thirty feet of water before the edge of his backyard. The bottom is mucky and soft and he keeps stubbing his toes on cypress roots.

"He's a boy," she had said. "Boys need dogs when they're twelve. It'll

2

give him someone to order around. Someone to bitch about his parents to."

That Saturday they drove to the Orange County SPCA and adopted a beagle/basset hound mix puppy. Lucy had wanted to call it "bagel."

"Get it?" she had asked. "Basset-beagle. Bagel."

"Jay, what do you want to call it?" Jack had asked his son.

Jay had shrugged, not wanting to get between his mother and his father. "I don't know yet."

"It needs a name," Lucy had said, becoming impatient. "You can't just say 'dog' all the time. 'Come here, dog.'"

Jay had sighed and rolled his eyes. His mother was always impatient or angry. Or his father was.

"I don't care," he had said. "Call him what you want to, I don't care."

For three days they had called the puppy "dog." Jay had finally named him "Hoover," because he always had his hound dog nose down in the carpet, searching for the lost and forgotten bits they had dropped there. When Lucy left Jack she left Hoover, too. He found out about it when he woke one morning to find her dumping clothes into a Hefty sack. He sat up and she walked out of the room.

Look at it this way, he told himself. When your wife leaves you, it's really a sort of beginning. The world is now livid with possibility. At six-thirty in the morning, in the dimness of his bedroom, it didn't sound convincing.

He lay back on the bed and listened to the sounds of Lucy's packing, the bang and rattle of her leave-taking. The sheets smelled musty. Lucy had been sleeping in the den, on a futon, for over a year. He'd been doing his own laundry for somewhat more than a year.

He could hear Hoover scratching and whining at the door of Jay's bathroom. Lucy had locked him up in there.

Ah, damn, he thought.

"I'm going now," Lucy said on the next pass through.

"I gathered."

"Jay's coming with me."

"Well," he said. "I guess I thought as much."

She looked at him for a long minute without saying anything.

"Is that it?" he asked.

Her jaw tightened. "You're damned right it is." She strode out of the room, jewelry box in hand.

"What about the dog?" Jack yelled after her.

"What about him?"

"He's Jay's, isn't he?"

"My mother doesn't want him in her house."

He got out of the bed and caught up with her as she was trying to open the door to the garage without dropping the jewelry box or the pair of pumps she had picked up with two fingers of her other hand, each finger inside a heel.

"Well, what the hell am I supposed to do with him?"

She managed to get the knob turned and pushed through the door with her shoulder. "Be original," she said without turning her head. "Take care of him."

He went back to Jay's room and let Hoover out of the bathroom. Hoover cowered and slinked out, looking as if he thought he had been locked up as punishment. Jack patted him reassuringly. He felt quite calm.

"Old son, you don't know what a shitty turn your life has just taken," he told the dog.

On impulse, he unbuckled Hoover's collar, with its clattering rabies tag and dog license. He made it to the front door with the collar in hand just as Lucy was starting the big Chevy Suburban they'd bought last year.

She saw him coming, and he could tell by the way her eyes narrowed that she was considering roaring off before he could get a chance to talk to Jay. Either that or she was considering running him down.

Jay rolled down his window as Jack came up. He looked a little scared, Jack thought. Probably of me. Probably thinks his old dad is going to do something insane and violent, like the dads on the news who go berserk and murder their families with shotguns before blowing their own collectively addled brains out.

4

Summoned like a genie by the thought, a seductively violent impulse grabbed him for a second before he could shake it off. Jay's eyes went a little wide, and Jack thought he must have sensed it.

He tried to be reassuring, but standing in his underwear in the steamy Florida morning, he felt conspicuous and threatening. He jingled the collar in his hand, feeling foolish, wondering what maudlin impulse had made him think Jay might want a memento of the dog he had to leave behind.

"I'll come visit," Jack told him.

"No," Lucy had said, without looking over at him.

"You can't keep me from seeing him," he said, talking across Jay. Jay closed his eyes, squeezing them shut.

"I'll bring him here."

"When?"

"I don't know. On weekends. Sundays."

"How often?

"I don't know." There was an edge of hysteria in her voice, which Jack felt the need to ignore.

"You're going to have to be more specific than that, sweetheart."

She slammed the gear lever into reverse and he jumped back to save his bare toes as the tires barked and the Suburban bumped out of the driveway.

"Great fucking move!" he yelled.

She jerked the truck into drive and peeled away down the blacktop, the tires screaming. He watched until it disappeared into the blinding distance of white-stuccoed ranch style houses.

Then he threw the dog collar after her. Across the street, his neighbor stared out at him from his living room window. The collar rang and clattered across the pavement, sounding like Christmas bells.

*

A wind picked up while he was swimming and now it blows through in anxious little gusts. The wet swimsuit clings and drools ice water down his legs. Hoover is standing expectantly by the door when he gets to the porch, doing the dance he does to let Jack know he needs to go.

Jack lets him out and stands shaking by the door while Hoover trots out and sniffs around the landscape timbers Lucy put in around the clumps of caladium.

"Do your business," Jack says to the dog. Hoover nuzzles a cypress knee.

"Now, dammit."

Hoover looks up and watches him, stupid and willful. Something swells up into Jack's chest like a breath of live steam. He takes a step toward the dog, and Hoover cowers away.

Jack rushes up and grabs him by the scruff of the neck and holds him belly-first against the base of a scrawny redbud tree. The dog whines and struggles and it is everything Jack can do to keep from balling up his fist and punching him, very hard. He wants to hurt him. He wants it very badly, the relief tangible and waiting, just on the other side of violence.

He lets Hoover go and the dog runs down to the edge of the water and squats there, looking back, whining and beating the muck with his tail, all submission and love.

"Christ," Jack says. He's bitten the inside of his cheek. He can taste the rusty flatness of the blood.

"Fucking, fucking dog." Calm down, he tells himself. There's no reason for this. For just an instant he can imagine Lucy there, in his face, telling him *control yourself, asshole.*

"It's not my fault," he tells her, but all of her contempt and a dose of his own hangs in the air like a stink.

★

The next morning he goes out into the too-bright Florida morning to get the newspaper from the driveway. It's already getting hot outside, the air over the street starting to crinkle and crawl in the distance. Hoover comes out with him and snuffles happily in the grass.

The paper is there once again, in its clean plastic bag, though he stopped paying for it two months ago. Somewhere, he thinks, there is a computer racking up points against me, just waiting. An almost pleasant needle of paranoia shivers though the top of his spine.

Noah, his neighbor across the street, looks up at Jack from the azaleas in his side yard. Jack waves and Noah waves back. Jack picks up the paper and shuffles back inside, feeling Noah's eyes on his back.

He remembers Hoover just as he closes the door. He opens it again and Hoover is already across the street, squatting in Noah's grass. Noah watches him, then glares across the street at Jack. Jack holds his hands palm up near his shoulders to signal What Can I Do Now?

Hoover finishes. Jack whistles and the dog trots back from the fatted green of Noah's lawn to the burned out brown of Jack's.

"Get over here," Jack says to him as he crosses the pavement, putting some anger in his voice for Noah's sake. Then he calls out, "Sorry." Noah shakes his head.

Hoover comes in and Jack closes the door. He can see Noah through the fist-sized, cut-glass window set at eye-level into one of the door panels. He looks at Hoover's shit, then he looks at Jack's house, expecting him, he guesses, to come trotting out with a newspaper to scoop the mess up.

"Guess again, pal." Hoover whines and wags his rear end, thinking Jack is talking to him. "You did fine," Jack tells him.

Noah disappears for a long moment, then comes back dragging a hose. He opens the nozzle and uses the stream to blast the feces off his lawn and out into the street. When he shuts the water off, his grass glistens in the sunlight as if it is strewn with tiny shards of broken glass.

★

Hoover's whining wakes him. He stands by the front door, waiting for Jack to let him out. He thinks about Noah, and leads the dog through the kitchen to the back.

He makes a cup of coffee by pushing a filter into a colander and running hot water from the tap over the grounds. It's weak and bitter and he pours a little milk in to cut the taste. Then he joins Hoover out in back.

The afternoon sun is high and blazing. He squints against the rhythmic silver flashes of light coming back from the water. Hoover is down by the dock, drinking from the lake. A breeze puffs up from off the water, smelling like mud and cocoa butter.

Two of the neighbors' kids, both girls, are standing on the end of the dock. As he watches, they dive in and begin to swim out toward a platform about fifty yards out, anchored there by his neighbor to the immediate south. Jack settles into a lawn chair left under one of the cypresses and watches the girls swim.

One, the youngest, dog-paddles intently. The other girl, maybe eight or nine, swims with considerably more grace, ducking under the water and swimming a few yards before she pops again to the surface. Her tank suit is a steely blue color that makes her look like a skinny porpoise in the water. She makes it out to the platform and heaves herself up on top. The boards must be hot, because she dances around a bit before sitting down on the edge, her feet in the brown water.

She sees Jack and waves. He recognizes her. She had been one of Jay's playmates for a while, until he decided he no longer wanted to associate with girls, especially not younger ones. Jack waves back. She starts to splash water up on the platform with one hand to cool it off and he is amazed that it had seemed so cold only twelve hours or so before.

He whistles at Hoover and the dog raises his head and looks at him, but doesn't come.

He settles deeper into the chair and drinks his coffee.

The air is charged with steam. It rolls up over the lawn from the lake, to settle over him like one of the prickly green-wool army quilts his grandmother had used on his bed when he was a kid. It feels comfortable and personal, as if it has come off the lake just to spread itself across him. He feels the sweat popping out all over, and he wishes he had thought to bring a beer out with him. As it is, it just seems too much effort to drag himself back up from the chair and into the dark and lonely air-conditioning.

Hoover wanders over after a while and settles down under the chair, his tongue lolling. Jack closes his eyes and tries to force a daydream about a girl with red hair he saw yesterday in the grocery. It doesn't gel, and he lets it go. Someone cranks up an outboard, and Jack listens to the throaty sputter of the motor counterpoint itself against the shrieking of the girls as they chase each other around on the diving platform.

Suburban bliss. Light splinters up from the lake. Hoover pants and the world hums with heat-pump fans.

★

Hoover whines and Jack wakes from a doze to find the older little girl standing between him and the lake. Hoover trots over and she kneels down so he can lick her face.

"Hi," she says.

"Hi back," he says.

"You sit out here a lot, don't you?"

"Not all that much. Just sometimes."

"My aunt Jean is going to get married."

Jack thinks about it. "Well, that's nice."

"My mom wants to know if you want to come."

He takes off his sunglasses. "Your mom wants me to come to your aunt's wedding?"

"Aunt Jean's getting married in our back yard. We just found out. My mom said to tell you that she's sorry she couldn't invite you in person herself, but she's getting everything ready and all. She said to tell you she's inviting the Garcias and the How-weirds, too, and some other people that live around here."

"The Garcias and the who?"

"The Howards. My mom calls them the How-weirds. 'How weird are the How-weirds?'"

It takes him a second to remember that Howard is Noah's last name. "Does your mom know my wife can't come?"

"Uh-huh. I think so." She squints at him. "Aunt Jean has to get married. She's going to have a baby. Her boyfriend's in college."

"Oh," he says. "When is this wedding?"

"Tomorrow, at six-thirty."

He thinks for a minute. "Tell your mother I'll try to come but I might not be able to make it. Tell her I said thank you, OK?"

"All right. Can your dog come, too? I don't think my mom'd mind if he came, too. Probably she wouldn't."

"I don't know. Maybe."

She clucks her tongue and Hoover jumps up, trying to get to her face. "I bet he likes cake."

"I'll bet he does, too. What's your name?"

She squints up at him. "Margaret Henson. My mom calls me Maggie."

"Maggie Henson. I like that. Maggie, I had a little girl like you once."

"Where'd she go?"

"She died." He looks at this little girl and says, "Somebody hit her with a car while she was riding her bicycle."

She thinks about it. "Wow. That's too bad."

"Yeah," he says, "it is." He is amazed at the lie he's just told, and mystified at why he's told it. He looks at this child, squatting with his dog pressed against her thin chest as she tries to hold him still and he nips at her pale and girl-simple face, and he wants for no real reason at all to cry.

"I guess you miss her, huh?"

"Yeah, I guess I do."

"Where's your little boy?" she asks.

"He moved away, to live with his mom. They live in St. Petersburg, now."

"Oh." She gives her attention back to Hoover. Then someone calls out and she looks up. Her mother is standing by the lake below their house. She's holding a cordless phone to her ear. He waves and she waves back. "I got to go. See you later, Mr. Lewis."

"Bye, Maggie," he says. He whistles to Hoover to get him to stay and Hoover wriggles in a circle, trying to watch Jack and the little girl at the same time, to see if Jack might relent and let him go after her.

"Come on, dammit," he tells the dog, and leads the way back up to the house. He opens the door and Hoover scoots into the dark kitchen, giving him a nervous glance as he goes by.

★

He sleeps through the early part of the afternoon and wakes up to the weighty, astricted grumble of thunder. He goes to the front door and watches the clouds roll in, blunt and gray. The first few heavy drops slap themselves flat on the concrete of the driveway, making perfect dark coins. The storm seems to hesitate for a second, the wind puffing in damp and fragrant from across the street, only slightly cooler than the air it displaces. Then the bottom drops out of the clouds and the rain comes down in black, drowning walls of water. The gutters fill in an instant and overflow. Water splatters up from the stoop onto the carpet where he stands. He steps out into it and shuts the door behind him.

At first it is like standing in a waterfall. The rainwater plasters his hair down and runs into his eyes. For a few seconds it is hard to breathe and the drops thunder like a blizzard of tiny fists pounding down on his head and the ground and the roof of the house.

He walks out into the middle of the yard. It feels extraordinary, intense and a little frightening, as if he is being softly thrashed by someone who might not know when to stop.

Then the torrent slackens, a little at first, then falling off suddenly into a warm steady shower. After a few minutes of that it simply quits.

He stands breathless and grinning at himself out in the muddy center of his lawn and listens to the rush of water start to taper off in the gutter spouts. One of them is loose and it rattles noisily in its stream. Thunder grumbles in a sodden and stubborn way off in the distance.

He wipes his face with his hands and looks around the neighborhood. Everyone else is still tucked away, weathering the storm. He walks out to the street, enjoying the way the muck squinches up between his toes. The storm drains suck and sputter with authority. The pavement steams and he wonders if, behind the water roar, it had hissed like an iron when the first sheet of rain had hit it.

Across the street Noah stares at him through his kitchen window. He waves and Noah closes the blinds.

How weird are the How-weirds? Certainly no weirder, he is sure, than Mr. Lewis across the street.

★

His neighbor's backyard has been decked out in yards of white crepe paper, strung from porch to water oak to palm tree. The dock is decorated too, and someone—Maggie, probably—has swum out to the diving platform and strung more white crepe paper and paper flowers around its edges. He wonders how she kept it all dry.

Maggie's mother flitters around her guests, seating people and ferrying their wedding gifts to a card table set up for the purpose. He feels bad about not having a gift, but she doesn't seem to notice that he's come empty-handed.

The wedding itself is quick and efficient. As soon as everyone seems seated, the music begins—Chopin played on an electric piano by the hostess. Then, as soon as everyone is sitting straight and paying attention, she drops into the march and Maggie and another little girl he doesn't recognize come down the aisle between the rows of folding chairs, tossing handfuls of flower petals from what look like Easter baskets. Then the bride follows, walking alone and wearing a white dress that doesn't look much like a wedding dress. If she is indeed pregnant, the dress hides it well.

The groom stands waiting for her beside the minister, looking decent enough, young and clean cut, wearing a black tux. The minister says his words, the couple kisses, and it is over.

Afterwards three or four of the groom's friends grab him and threaten to throw him in the lake. The bride stands to one side, surrounded suddenly by her sister and her sister's guests, all wishing her well. He wanders up to the porch, where a bar and a buffet have been set up on folding tables. Noah from across the street is already there, loading up a plate. He blinks, then says, "Hello."

"Hi, Noah," Jack says. Noah seems embarrassed. He waves his paper plate a bit. "Nice wedding," he says.

As the evening settles into gray, everyone brings folding chairs down to the concrete pad near the lake and eats together, balancing the paper plates on napkin-covered knees. The bride and groom duck into the house and come back a while later in shorts and T-shirts. Both T-shirts have the same logo, a pink pig, the size of a fist, lying on his stomach on a brown streak of airbrushed sand, sunglasses perched on his snout. Printed underneath the logo is the legend, "Bacon on the Beach." The newlyweds hold hands but don't look much at each other.

When Jack is finished he takes his plate off to the trash barrel and drops it in. Noah is there, standing behind the barrel, one hand in a pocket, one holding a drink, watching everyone else eat now that he's through.

"Nice wedding," he says again.

"I noticed," Jack says, then thinks he ought to be friendlier, even to Noah, given the nature of the event. "Your wife couldn't make it?"

"No." He looks at Jack and takes a drink of his cocktail. "No, she couldn't."

"Oh," Jack says. He's noticing for the first time how really old Noah is. He's always assumed he's late fortyish, seeing him working in his yard. He looks older now. His face is leathery and he has a pencil mustache cut straight across his upper lip, a forties detective movie-looking thing.

Noah feels he has to explain. "She isn't too good out with people anymore. Mostly, we stay home."

"Oh," Jack says again. "I'm sorry to hear that."

He shrugs. "It's OK. We get along."

The post-sunset gray of the sky has darkened into blue-black. The concrete pad sits in a scalloped pool of light from the floodlights. Noah follows as Jack walks back to his chair. He pulls a vacant chair up and settles in next to Jack. The moon has started to rise on one side, still a thin sliver, needling up through the trees with one narrow pale horn. The water below picks up all the light and breaks it into pieces, jelly-shaking it around on the little ripples.

People have started to drift away from the reception. He notices that the bride and groom in their pig T-shirts are gone. Maggie Henson comes bouncing up from the lake into the light, wearing her steely blue tank suit. Her hair is dry, though, and he assumes she hasn't been in the water. She sees him and comes over. She gives Noah a little wave and he nods to her but keeps talking.

"Where's your dog?"

"He's at home."

"How come?"

"Oh," he says, "I don't think he likes weddings much, after all."

"Oh," she says, not sounding particularly disappointed. She pulls a chair up beside him, on the side away from Noah, then sits in it with a little backwards hop that makes the aluminum legs jerk grittily an inch or two across the concrete.

"Thinking of taking a swim?" he asks.

She leans forward in her chair, letting her legs swing back and forth underneath it. "I was."

"You changed your mind?"

"No. My mom won't let me. I was going to go out and get the flowers off the float, but she said I could do it tomorrow, because it's dark now."

He thinks about his own excursions into the midnight lake. "Makes sense to me," he tells her.

"What's that?" Noah asks, leaning out from his chair. Jack explains.

"Christ Almighty, I would hope not," Noah says. He shakes a finger at Maggie, the way an old maid schoolteacher might in a TV movie. "Last thing you need to be doing is swimming in that lake, especially when it's already night out."

"Why's that?" someone asks, a heartbeat before Jack does, her tone considerably less sarcastic than his would have been. She's a young woman, early twenties, Jack thinks, and he wonders if she is a friend of the bride.

Noah holds up one finger to say "wait a minute," then stands up from his chair and walks without another word off into the darkness between the Henson's house and the next.

"How weird are the How-weirds?" Jack says to Maggie. She giggles. He sees that her mother has positioned herself up near the porch and is saying goodnight and shaking hands as people leave. She seems to be having a good time, smiling a lot.

Noah comes back, carrying what looks to be a spotlight and a big, brick-sized battery. He sits down and starts hooking the light's wires up to the battery's terminals.

"This is a Q-beam," he says when he's finished. He holds it up to show them, a lens case about six inches across on top of a pistol-grip handle that trails a coil of wire. "Quartz-halogen, brighter'n hell. Real powerful. Now look."

They look. He points the spotlight at the lake and snaps it on. A bright, solid-looking beam jumps out and becomes an oblong on the water beyond the dock. He holds the spotlight low, down below his knees, and sweeps it out across the water like a searchlight, as if he's looking for something. After a second he holds it still.

"See?" he says.

"What?" Jack squints out to where the light is pointed. Then he sees it. Two pinpoints of red, maybe a hundred yards out, sparkling in the spotlight's beam like tiny, faraway car taillights.

"See 'em?" Noah asks again.

"Yes," the girl who might be a friend of the bride says.

"Yeah, sure," Jack says. "What are they?"

"'Gator eyes."

"You're not serious."

"No kidding," the girl says. She sounds intrigued. "A real alligator?"

"Yup. As real as they come. They're all out there." He plays the light out across the water again, sweeping from left to right. Jack squints, watching. He counts six separate sets of eyes glinting back at them. Most of them are way out, scattered along the far shore, but some of them are closer, little demon eyes glaring back.

"Those are just the ones looking at us," Noah says.

Jack feels a shrinking tingle in his bowels. "I didn't think about 'gators being out here, in the city almost. There weren't that many around when I was a kid, not even in the boonies. Not that I remember."

"Those suckers are everywhere now, bud. Big lizards all over the place, like in a movie, since they got protected back in the seventies. Or sixties. I don't remember. Lots of 'gators around now—people hittin' 'em with their cars out on the freeway, too, like speed bumps. I've seen 'em. They don't stay out there long, though, the dead ones. People pick them up, take them home. Alligator tail's like gourmet food, these days. Fifteen, twenty bucks a pound."

"Gourmet road kill," the girl says. "I like it."

"'Gators don't mess with people usually," Jack says. He's rationalizing, trying to make himself feel better. It's true, though, at least he thinks it is. Still, his skin crawls at the thought. How close has he come to one of those things out there, late at night, thinking he was alone? He has vision of a mouth, wide like one of those big machines that crushes cars but full of teeth, pulling him down.

"No," Noah concedes, "they don't. Not full grown people. But I'm damned if I'd let a kid out there. And dogs. They eat dogs. I'd watch that one of yours, boy." He wags a finger at Jack.

"I'll do that," Jack says. He feels a sudden rise of irritation at Noah. It isn't that he knows things Jack doesn't and should, having grown up not sixty miles from Noah's smooth, green, overindulged front lawn. It's that he is right and Jack is wrong again, or stupid, or worse. Jack thinks then that he must have known all along about the alligators, somewhere underneath. Maybe that had been one of the appeals of the swimming, the danger he knew about and didn't acknowledge. Now it is out there and he'll even have to be careful about letting Hoover take a shit too close to the water.

It doesn't matter. Noah is playing the spoiler, full of good advice and high-sentence, and what Jack really wants at the moment is to belt him one, just to shake up his smugness. Give it to him, right in the teeth. Polonius behind the curtain with a rapier stuck through his liver. Fucking know-it-all old man. He can feel the knot of muscle alongside his jaw spasm.

Maggie leans in close and whispers conspiratorially, "I've seen them before, the alligators. Sometimes they swim right by the float. Don't tell my mom."

The girl looks at Jack, her eyebrows raised, and laughs. "Can you beat it?" Her teeth look yellow in the light and glossy, like a row of corn.

He lets it go. He sits back in his chair. "No, I can't," he says, "not with a stick."

Noah makes a pass with the Q-beam again. Far out on the water red eyes light up and twinkle like malevolent little stars.

★

16

He's not as surprised, he thinks, as he ought to be when he wakes up and someone is in bed with him. She's lying on her side next to him, her head tucked under, and he has to lever himself up on an elbow, peel back the comforter and crane over her to see who she is: the girl from the wedding, asleep and achingly young on his bed, wearing the same Bacon on the Beach T-shirt the bride and groom had worn. She must have had it on under her blouse. He figures it's some sort of group thing with them, like gang colors.

He settles back and listens to the magnified quiet in the house, the tiny ticks and groans of clocks and things shifting and settling into themselves in darkness. Then he slips carefully out of the bed and goes into the bathroom. His swim trunks are on the towel rod inside the shower and they are dry and stiff when he pulls them on, balancing on one foot at a time on the slick, cool tile.

The dog bumps his tail against the wall when he comes into the kitchen and he hisses at him to keep quiet. He opens the door carefully and takes a deep breath. It's maybe three A.M., foggy outside, the air glowing a luminescent white. Everything is damp and clean smelling and loud with the sound of drops falling off of the trees onto the grass.

He wades slowly out into the water. The water is chillier than he'd expected. He launches himself out into it. He swims for a few minutes in a steady freestyle, warming up, feeling the blood start to flow. When he judges he's halfway across the lake, he flips over onto his back and drifts. The fog hangs low over the water, glowing slightly with the light from the city and the streetlights. Just the fog and the crisp sounds of his own movements in the water. Womblike, he thinks. No, not womblike. More like how he might imagine an afterlife, cool and dark and fertile with the punky smell of the lake water.

But even as he thinks that, he feels the terrible isolation of it. He lets his legs sink and treads water. All he can see is fog and darkness and he's a little unsure in which direction the house lies. It doesn't really matter, he knows. The lake is small; swim in any direction and he'll come up on shore pretty quickly. Still, it's an uncomfortable feeling. Noah's 'gators surround him in their hidden reptilian hunger, ready to pull him under.

He's amazed that the thought doesn't scare him much. He forces himself to recall the stories he's heard again and again, part of the suburban myth of a city where almost every neighborhood has some kind of lake. The skier who skied into a huge knot of mating water moccasins. The fisherman who fell out of his boat and got tangled in an old fishing line and struggled until he got so wrapped up in line and hooks that he couldn't swim and drowned. All bullshit, or mostly. Nothing's ever as bad as people make it out to be.

He takes a deep breath and then another, feeling his lungs fill.

Then he hears Hoover bark nearby, and a woman's voice singing the single broad syllable of his name in an unwavering, anxious soprano. The wedding girl, shivering, he imagines, thin and naked under her pig T-shirt. She must have woken, missed him. He must have left the door open. Hoover would've gone down to the water, looking for him, sniffing the grass. She keeps calling and he listens to her voice for a moment, cutting its clear way through fog. Her voice is a prayer on the water, an appeal to his solitude. He takes a slow stroke and turns so he's floating on his back, hidden in the lake's weedy ease. At the far end of the lake where the fog has started to rise, the stars seem to rumble through the horizon's thin blue lip. He imagines the girl on the shore waiting for him, thinking of him, her arms across her chest, holding herself unselfconsciously, as no one else will ever hold her.

"Hey," he calls out to her. His voice echoes strangely across the midnight water. She doesn't answer, but he hears sudden splashing and he thinks she has decided for some reason to join him out in the water. He waits, but it's Hoover who comes swimming up, paddling frantically, his narrow head just above the reflected flickering of the porch lights on the water's surface.

"Ah, hell," Jack says. He's thinking about the alligators again, and what a tempting mouthful Hoover must make, flailing away in the water. He swims hard toward the dog but Hoover veers away from him. Jack can feel his temper flare, but he reins it in and angles over to intercept the dog. He catches up and grabs Hoover by the scruff of the neck and accidentally shoves him under the water in the process. Hoover comes up twisting and yelping and it's everything Jack can do to keep a grip on the slippery, wet fur. He sidestrokes back toward the shore with the dog struggling hard both to swim and to break free. When he reaches shallow water, Jack pitches the dog up toward the shore and Hoover lands with a splash a few feet out and scrambles up onto the grass, where he stops and shakes himself. Jack trudges up out of the lake after him, the mud sucking at his feet.

The girl is sitting on his lawn chair with her feet tucked up under her and her T-shirt stretched down over her knees.

"Weird," she says. Hoover runs up and jumps on her and she rubs his head and pushes him back down. When Jack walks up to her, he can see two brown muddy streaks from Hoover's paws across the picture of the pig on the front of her shirt.

"How weird are the How-weirds," Jack says.

"Huh?"

"Nothing," he tells her. She puts her feet down and the shirt slides up to her waist. She puts her hand out and he takes it and pulls her up out of the chair. She comes into his arms and he thinks that he doesn't even remember her name. He kisses her with something that's pretty close to desperation. She smells like beer and sex and sleep.

"Jesus, you're wet," she says. She bends her head back from him, holds him off a bit. "What were you doing out there?"

"Swimming with the 'gators," he tells her.

"I get it," she says, "I know what that's like."

He doesn't know what she means and then he thinks that he does. She's here with him, after all, taking the kind of chances that people probably shouldn't take. Hoover barks and Jack looks over his shoulder to see him down by the water again. He's looking out into the lake and Jack can feel the eyes out there, little and red and reptilian, watching for a chance. He shivers and says, "Hoover! Get back from there."

The girl whose name he doesn't even know says, "I'll bet you're freezing. She comes in close again and he can feel the warmth of her through her T-shirt. She puts her head against his chest. "Maybe we ought to go back in and warm you up."

He almost says *sure* and then he almost says *no thanks* but ends up saying nothing at all until the silence gets strange and uncomfortable and she shifts in his arms to look up at him. He doesn't meet her eyes. He's thinking about being alone. He's thinking about how much he's going to miss swimming late at night, how in his heart he's already granted the lake to the alligators. He thinks, in a moment we'll go back inside. I'll go back and talk to this girl, ease her out of my house and my life. I'll go back in and keep on living the life I've been living.

He wants to tell this girl something, to warn her. But a cold breeze blows across his back and Hoover whines to be let back into the house. *It's not my fault,* he wants to say. He takes her hand, gently, the way he might take a daughter's hand if he had a daughter, to take her inside, sit her down, give her some good advice. *Be careful, watch for alligators, stay away from men like me.*

But he's not her father, and her hand is warm in his, and he guides her up the slope of the grass to the house. He opens the door and Hoover rushes in past them, his nails clicking madly on the tile.

"Guess he's glad to get back," Jack says.

"Well, it's scary out there," she says, and presses herself into his arms again, willing and soft in the dark kitchen.

"It's scary everywhere," he tells her.

"I'm not scared," she says, and he marvels at how lovely she is, how confident and young. When he pulls the T-shirt off over her head, he can feel the cold clamminess of the material where it has soaked up the lake water on his skin. He can smell the lake on her, transferred to her body from his own. It smells, he imagines, like the alligators do. He wants to do something crazy, drag her outside to the lake, make love to her in the water and the fetid, soft mud, in the glare of cold eyes everywhere, watching.

But he puts his hands on her hips and turns her. Then with his palm pressed against the warm reassurance of her backside, he guides her into the safe inner rooms of his home.

RUNNING AWAY

It was Donny McLaughlin who taught Fisher how to run away, not suddenly, but with careful style. Donny had been doing it since he was six, when he stowed away in the backseat of the car of a mechanic from Lakeland who had come to his father's salvage yard to pick up a manifold for a '58 Chevy half-ton pickup. With Fisher along, Donny became even more ambitious. They'd thumbed rides with fruit trucks and been brought home by state troopers, hitched freight trains to Lakeland and St. Petersburg and been brought home by deputy sheriffs.

Finally, Walker, Fisher's old man, had had enough. He wasn't about to put up with having the sheriff or some other representative of municipal order showing up at his doorstep with his errant fourteen-year old son in tow, and had decided to send Fisher to the Polk Institute for Boys in Bartow, where they'd teach Fisher a little military discipline and self-respect. Fisher thought that they had done a fine job of it on his older brother, Jarl. One early June morning, the summer after Jarl graduated from the Polk Institute, he had driven his new Chevy Impala off a highway bridge and into the Peace River, where a sheriff's department diver found him, still buckled in, two days later. The police said it was an accident because it was foggy out and Jarl was driving fast, but Fisher believed Jarl simply couldn't live any longer with what the institute had made of him.

Fisher had been at the Polk Institute for less than a day before he'd come to the unshakable conviction that if he stayed there, he, too, would certainly die or be so crushed in spirit he might as well be dead. A few minutes after midnight he sat up in his lower bunk on his olive-drab blanket and dressed himself silently in the one set of "civvies" he'd been allowed to pack. Then he walked to the front door of the barracks where the Officer of the Day had fallen asleep at his desk, and out into the night.

Fisher had ridden the freights that pulled through Mascotte Grove more times than he could count. The trains moved at a crawl from the sidings outside the juice plant to the far side of town before picking up speed just beyond the salvage yard owned by Donny's father, and so Fisher simply walked the quarter-mile from the Polk Institute for Boys to the tracks where they passed behind the packing house and waited for the two o'clock train to grind by. He sat on one of the hard cold rails and waited for the telltale vibration to start up through the seat of his pants to tell how a train was pulling off one of the sidings and coming his way.

A hurricane was stirring lazily off in the gulf. He knew this because the cadet colonel had announced it at morning formation so the corps would know they'd be volunteering for sandbag duty should the necessity arise. A cool drizzle started up while he waited, and he sat, miserable and sleepy, a runnel of water dribbling down off his chin, trying to stay awake enough to plan the rest of his escape. It was Monday and Donny wouldn't have much money after the weekend, and now it was raining, too, so Fisher figured Donny would be home, or at least near his daddy's trailer house, sleeping in one of the junked cars. Donny didn't stay in the house itself much because he wanted to stay clear of his daddy as much as he could. Fisher could respect that. He did what he could to stay clear of his own father. He was planning to stay awfully clear from here on out. So clear it would make even Walker wonder.

He had only the one set of clothes on his back, and those were wet, but he had some money, fifty dollars his mother had given him just before Walker had driven him over to the institute. One thing Fisher was sure of—leaving Mascotte Grove would be easy enough. It was keeping some well-meaning dimwit from bringing them back that was the trick.

He felt a vibration start up underneath him and down the line he could hear a shriek as a wheel on one of the freight cars rubbed the rail. He stood up and backed off from the tracks so that he was hidden in the shadow under a willow tree. After a while the train loomed up, its single headlight searching the woods as it groaned and squealed its way around the bend. Fisher waited for the engine to pass, the engineers framed in the light of the side windows. He waited for a boxcar with an open door but the train crept by, each car shut tight, and when he could see the light in the turret on the caboose coming around the bend he came out of the willow's shadow and ran alongside the train. On the back of one of the cars was a ladder. He grabbed at one of the round metal rungs, caught it, and jumped. He climbed carefully up to the center of the ladder and locked his elbows around a rung and clung there in the rumbling darkness, trembling and so happy he could hardly breathe.

Fisher jumped off the freight where a dirt road crossed the tracks about a quarter of a mile above the McLaughlin's salvage yard. He and Donny had learned the hard way that leaving a moving train, especially in the dark, was best done at intersections because you always fell, and it was far better to fall on the relatively soft sand of a country road than on the gravel skirt that bordered the tracks for ten feet on either side everywhere else. Fisher still managed to land on a bit of broken bottle that cut through his jeans and left a stinging crescent-shaped cut just below his knee. After the train was past, he limped the quarter mile down the tracks to Donny's place.

Donny was relatively easy to find. Fisher stood under the window of the room Donny shared sometimes with two of his older brothers, but decided against tapping on the pane out of fear it might be Daryl who came to the window. Daryl liked to slap Fisher on the back of the head with his open palm, hard enough to make Fisher's teeth click together. He was a tall, narrow boy with stooped shoulders who always smelled of grease and gasoline and who had dropped out of school in the seventh grade to strip cars with his daddy in the salvage yard. He thought Fisher was a lucky little rich bastard who needed to be brought down a notch when an opportunity presented itself. Fisher didn't feel much like presenting him with one.

It had started to rain again in a languid sort of way, fat drops falling with a ping like tiny ball-peen hammers on the acre-and-a-half of rusting metal gathered around the trailer. Fisher was starting to miss his bunk at the institute, just a little bit. He walked around the trailer to the front, where the newest wrecks were lined up in a ragged row under the sallow light from an arc lamp mounted high on a telephone pole. The car on the end was a Lincoln, a long, square-shouldered barge of a car, its front end crushed inwards in a deep V where it had been run into a tree or pole of some sort. He tried the door and it opened with a stiff popping groan. He leaned in and said, "Hey, you in there?"

Donny rose up from the darkness that lay tucked over the deep velour of the Lincoln's long front seat. His eyes were still closed and he looked pale in the reflected light from the arc lamp. Fisher wondered if he were still asleep. "Shit," Donny said.

"Are you awake?" Fisher asked. Donny blinked and squinted. "No," he said. "What the hell do you want?"

"If I'd been a hobo or something, you'd be dead right now."

"Shit," Donny said, and yawned. "'Bos don't kill anyone."

"Like you'd know."

Donny shrugged. "I ain't dead yet. Besides, there's a hurricane coming. Nobody with any sense goes out in a hurricane."

The rain was starting to come down harder, the pinging of the drops on the acres of wrecked cars moving from a slow, sad dirge up-tempo to something like a listless waltz. He climbed into the Lincoln beside Donny and shut the door just as the sky let loose in a dark rush. Donny lit a candle and tilted it so that wax dripped onto the dashboard, then he set the candle in the hot wax and held it for a second until the wax hardened enough to hold the candle upright. The wax smelled greasy and old-tirish on the dash's hard plastic. They sat a while without talking, listening to the sudden torrent batter the car roof like something desperate to get inside with them. Then the rain eased as suddenly as it began into a fine shower. Underneath the odor of the candle wax the car smelled musty, though it looked on the inside like any other car Fisher had been in. He somehow always felt that a junkyard car should be different, changed, so that it didn't seem any longer like something quite so familiar and functional. It should feel dead. But none of them ever did. Even the ones so rusted out that the rain came through the holes in the roof felt like someone had just stepped away from them, and soon enough they'd be back on the road.

"Did someone get killed in this car?"

Donny shrugged. "I don't know. Maybe. Look at this, though." He reached down between his knees under the seat, pressing the side of his face against the steering wheel. He dragged out a stack of three or four magazines and placed them on the seat between Fisher and himself. They looked slick in the flickering candlelight, waxy and new.

"Where the hell did you get those?"

"Daryl stole a whole load of 'em from the store."

"Check this out." Donny opened the top magazine to the centerfold and folded out a tan, blond girl sitting sideways on a saddle balanced on a bale of hay. She was wearing a cowboy hat and a leather vest with tassels, and she had her arms crossed with her upper arms pressing against the sides of her breasts so that they swelled unbelievably close in the camera's eye.

"Jesus," Fisher said.

"Pretty cool, huh?"

"Damn." The word fell like a drop from his bottom lip.

"Yeah," Donny added, "Goddamn."

"Look," Fisher said, "I'm out of here. I can't stand that frigging school any more."

Donny looked at the girl another long moment before folding her up and closing the magazine. "What you want me to do about it, son?"

"I thought maybe you'd like to go, too."

"Hell, why would I want to go anywhere? I'm the goddamn king of the Seminoles right here. Got a Lincoln road car to live in."

"Funny guy," Fisher told him.

"You bet," Donny said.

Getting Donny's things out of the trailer took time. Donny went alone, creeping through the tangled darkness inside to avoid waking his parents or his brothers. The trailer house was not a tidy place, and Donny had to be very careful. By the time he'd gathered his things into a trash bag and gotten back to the door, Fisher could hear the five o'clock train's horn moaning in the near distance as it crossed the river road a half-mile away.

"Get a move on!" he hissed at Donny, and Donny eased the trailer door shut, holding the knob turned so that the latch wouldn't click as he closed it. They ran together at full tilt down to the crossing. The engineer didn't bother to blow his horn as the train approached. Fisher saw the engine's light loom and cross the road, and the train followed, clanking and squealing, the boxcars dark and solid as bricks. The first ten or eleven cars were closed tight. A few flatcars followed, empty and open to the moonlight, and then a few dark tankers filled, Fisher imagined, with pesticides. Two open-topped hopper cars filled with phosphate rock from the pits out near Bartow. More flatcars. Fisher could see the light at the top of the caboose coming, and only a few more cars left, none of them boxcars.

"No boxcars!" he yelled to Donny. The cars clacked and squealed over his voice. Donny pointed to a flatcar three cars ahead of the caboose and started to trot alongside the train. Fisher followed, gravel shifting under his feet as he ran. When the flatcar drew up beside them, Donny threw his bag on, then leapt up onto the car's wooden floor, landing flat on his belly, his legs dangling until he found a handhold and drew himself up. Fisher took two more strides, afraid to get too close because he might trip on the end of a railroad tie, and dove, his arms outstretched. He landed on the car's platform, the metal edge pressed into his stomach just above his hips. He teetered for a second, his fingers pressed into the platform's wooden floor, his legs hanging out over the side. Something bumped hard against the toe of his shoe where his feet hung down in the darkness near the ground and he was pitched sideways, his fingers slipping across the boards. Then Donny grabbed him by the elbow and shoulder and hauled him up onto the car.

Donny was laughing. "Almost lost you there, boy!"

"Christ on a crutch," Fisher said.

"Bet your ass," Donny said. "Now we're havin' fun."

★

After about another hour, the first olive hint of sunrise started to thin out the darkness. The train passed through intersections where automobiles waited for it to go by and Donny and Fisher had to press themselves down against the flatcar's platform to keep from being silhouetted by the headlights. Fisher looked up to the sky growing blond on the horizon and knew they'd have to move before daylight was full and truly up, because sure as hell some busybody would see two boys riding a freight toward Atlanta and would call the police just as soon as he or she got near enough a telephone to do it. Whatever else Fisher knew about human nature, he was confident in his conviction that very few people had the strength of will to mind their own business.

Donny led the way, walking in a careful crouch down the length of the flatcar to where the couplings held the flatcar and a hopper car together like two clenched fists. Donny reached an exploratory foot out into the gap between the cars and touched the couplings carefully with the toe of his shoe, then gave the foot some weight and shifted suddenly over in one step so that he was standing against the ladder welded to the sloping end of the hopper car. He edged over to give Fisher room.

Fisher reached down with his foot so that the toe of his tennis shoe sat lightly on the line where the couplings overlapped. He could feel the couplings shift under his foot as the cars swayed, a nervous wriggling like tree limbs rubbing together in a wind. There was enough light now that he could see he the darker shadows of the railroad ties blinking by in the dimness below. He leaned forward and for a precarious instant felt himself suspended on one foot over the real thing, death itself, rattling and sparking its oblong eye below him as he stood over it on a steady leg, balanced like a crane. He stepped forward and grabbed the ladder beside Donny's head, then put his foot on the rung and led the way up.

Over the top of the hopper car's end wall, the wind blew insistently, picking up bits of grit from the phosphate pebbles piled up to within a foot of the car's top edge. Fisher climbed over onto the rock and crouched there while Donny came up. Donny clambered over the car's blunt steel lip and fell in beside Fisher. He was laughing, his eyes narrow against the wind and grit.

"Yee-hah," he shouted.

All morning the sky roiled with clouds but there wasn't much rain. Fisher wondered if the hurricane had decided to miss Florida after all and head off to Texas, maybe. He kept himself tucked down below the leading edge of the car so the wind didn't pester him and so he couldn't be seen by anyone watching the train. Donny fell asleep, but Fisher was thinking, which was a habit that pretty much kept him from ever getting enough rest. Most of his running away he hadn't thought much about actually *staying* away; mostly, he'd been just going with Donny, who couldn't have ever cared less whether he came back to Mascotte Grove or not. Mostly, Fisher hadn't considered very far beyond the leaving, the livid sense of release like something visceral letting go when he and Donny crossed the county line and the world opened out complete before them in its distances.

In the afternoon the overcast sky darkened as the train moved north, the citrus groves in their dark green formations across the sand hills petering out and giving way to miles of soggy-looking marsh filled with sawgrass and egrets, then pine flats and palmetto jungle. The train stopped twice to pick up cars and Fisher and Donny squeezed in against the side of the car and lay in the phosphate rubble waiting for the train to move again or for a face to appear over the side of the car, someone checking for hobos or runaways. Toward evening they could see rain ahead, heavy dark streaks like the folds in a curtain crossing the tracks a mile or two in front of the engine.

"It's about to break loose," Donny said matter-of-factly.

"Should we get off?" The train was moving slowly along a siding. The woods on either side were thick and impenetrable-looking, heavy with shadow.

"Shit, I don't know. Where do you suppose we are?"

"Maybe near Gainesville. I don't know."

"Gainesville, hell. There ain't no woods like this in Gainesville. I'll bet we ain't even in Florida. Maybe south Georgia. Thomasville, maybe."

"Well, what do we do?"

A few big raindrops began to slap against the phosphate. "Cut, I guess. We're going to drown here. We can get back to the main tracks and pick up another train that's got boxcars, maybe."

"Hell, I guess so." A voice in his head complained *you don't get off a train in the middle of nowhere and just start walking*, but he ignored it. Donny threw his bag over the side and it hit the gravel and rolled down to the high weeds at the margin. Fisher climbed down the ladder and stood for a moment on the coupling, watching the shadowy woods. Then Donny touched him on the back and he jumped down onto the gravel and slid. Donny whooped and jumped down beside him, spraying gravel as he ran to keep from falling down.

They watched the train creak and spark down the siding. Off in the distance, under the gray streaks of rain, Fisher could just see a pair of squat towers beside a hill of dirt or sand. Back down the tracks, the way the train had come, was just more woods. Thunder rumbled.

"C'mon," Donny said, and started back up the tracks toward his bag. They jogged between the tracks, running slowly so as to stay on the ties. Fisher could hear the rain now, a rushing susurrus coming up fast. On one side of the tracks he saw an old, shattered wooden crate and three or four worn tires, and beyond them an opening in the brush and trees leading down a shallow embankment. Lightning flashed so close the world went sudden-white. The thunderclap knocked him to his knees. He thought he had shrieked, but he wasn't sure. Donny crouched down beside him.

"Holy shit," Donny yelled.

The rain swept over them in a soaking curtain. Fisher picked up Donny's bag where he'd dropped it and started toward the open place in the brush. The rain had already turned the embankment greasy with mud and he slid down, crouched on his heels, one hand out to keep him from pitching backwards. At the bottom of the slope was a shallow, mud-bottomed creek, its near bank bare and streaked with the hard slender backs of exposed tree roots. On its far side was a clearing beaten out in the brush and trees. There was a mattress to one side of the clearing, rusty stains showing where the springs lurked under the cover, and a fire ring made out of broken pieces of cinder block. Three railroad ties were arranged around it like low benches and everywhere in the clearing there was garbage, scrap lumber, food wrappers, soggy cardboard boxes, and beer and liquor bottles, some of them still in brown paper sacks twisted tight to their necks. Sitting alone in the brown water at the edge of the stream was a softly rotting, bright red Hi Ho cracker box.

The rain drummed in the trees overhead where it gathered in the thick foliage and began to come through in fat, musky drops. A mockingbird dove into the clearing, lit on one of the railroad ties, cocked its head at them, and hopped down into the fire ring. Then Fisher moved and it spread its wings and flicked off into the trees on the other side of the stream.

Donny picked up the edge of a moldy-looking piece of plyboard and Fisher helped him prop it up into a lean-to with some stubby lengths of two-by-four. They crouched underneath it in the earthworm smell and watched the little creek swell up with runoff. Rivulets of water crept under the plyboard with them so that they sat, miserable in their own puddles, and listened to the night come down in its loud and lonely voices.

★

Fisher woke when the creaking of the little frogs stopped suddenly enough that even in his sleep he knew something had changed. The night had gone blue with light creeping down through the trees and all he could hear was dripping. He sat up shivering, his clothes soaked through and clammy against his skin and waited for the frogs to start up again, without really even knowing that that was what he was waiting for. He eased out from beneath the plyboard and stood listening. Nothing. He stooped to shake Donny awake and heard the soft-pulp sound of someone setting a booted foot down in mud. It was a distinct sound, as identifiable and clear above the patter of dripping water as a shout.

Donny woke with a gasp and Fisher could feel the entire clearing go tense. Fisher stood again. He peered down into the deeper darkness by the creek. A shape hunched and solid resolved itself against the lighter shadows, standing close to the bank.

"Who's there?" The voice boomed under the trees like a bottle dropped into a steel trash can. Fisher froze.

"Shit," Donny whispered.

"I asked you," the voice said. The sound of it was catarrhal, rumbling. Fisher imagined an enormous toad. The shadow by the creek began to rise, misshapen and two-headed, feet slapping in the wet clay as it climbed up the shallow bank toward them.

"I said who the hell's there." Not two heads, Fisher realized. The light seemed to condense, clarify one more degree so that he could see. It was carrying a truck tire over its shoulder, arm through the center as if it were lugging an inner tube on the beach.

Donny was beside him. Fisher hadn't seen him move, all of his attention focused forward, but now he saw Donny take a single long step forward, the way a pitcher steps into his pitch, and throw something that Fisher's eye couldn't follow. There was a scream, amazingly high. Then he was running and Donny was just ahead, profiled against the brighter opening in the trees where the tracks were. He was running and something in the shadows grabbed him, pulled his feet out from under him so that he fell, his breath knocked suddenly and painfully out.

He'd fallen over the tire. He could see it; he was lying on his stomach, his breath coming hard. And he could see the hobo as well. It was a woman, he realized. She moaned. Her face was no more than five feet from his own and he could see her. Everything else in the clearing was still blurred with half-light but he could see her face. She was very fat. She was dirty and she was crying. There was blood on her forehead and cheek and she was crying, an awful sound, her eyes squeezed shut and her hands hovering on either side of her face like fat, pale moths.

Fisher was startled when he saw her; for a long moment he couldn't move, he could only watch her weep. He could feel water soaking through his already damp shirt from the puddle he was lying in. He could hear Donny yelling somewhere but it seemed abstract and far away. He had the curious feeling that nothing could ever reach him there, that so long as he didn't move the simple distance between himself and the woman would remain inviolable forever. The woman moaned once more and Fisher's heart seemed to start again with a jerk. Her hands settled onto her face, her fingers fluttering at the wound on her forehead. Fisher stood up and her eyes opened and focused on him and he looked at her looking at him and he ran, not looking back, out to where Donny waited, looking scared, standing on a tie between the rails, another rusty two-pound railroad spike in his hand ready to throw.

"Come on," Donny said, "let's get the hell out of here." Fisher followed him, running down the tracks. It took an hour to get to the main line. Fisher wondered the whole way about what he had seen in her face when she had opened her eyes, not what he'd expected, not rage, not the recognition of the world's great inequity he'd was sure he would see, but a simple blankness as wide as the sky silver with stars. Nothing at all but pain and a certain open wonder reflected out at him as if from a mirror. It was the sort of thing that could make you begin to doubt that anything at all was possible anymore, or that it ever had been. It was the sort of thing, he began at that moment to realize, that running away was all about, knowing from the first step that you'll never in your whole life go far enough to get away.

★

The wind had picked up enough that the tops of the trees were slashing restlessly back and forth across a sky that had grown suddenly less yellow and more dark and ominous. Fisher felt a strange feeling of lightness, as if the lowering clouds were gently pulling him upward toward themselves. He felt he had to walk carefully, keeping low to the ground. He had heard that hurricanes were like this, the hard weather coming and going as it swept its trailing arms about, but this seemed different and scary. Donny had gotten ahead and Fisher caught up with him just as he was pulling apart the strands of barbed wire off to one side of the tracks. Beyond the fence was a field. In the center of the field, surrounded by its own chain-link fence, was a water tower, STARKE emblazoned in orange letters across the broad belly of its tank. Underneath that was written, in black spray paint, CLASS OF '81.

Donny stood up on the far side of the barbed wire and pointed up at the tower, grinning.

"Hell, no!" Fisher shouted at him, and stopped. Donny shouted back, but Fisher lost the words in the roaring of the wind. It blew constantly now, full of dust and a damp sea smell. "Dumbass!" he shouted to Donny and felt a wildness pass through him then, a fierce exultation. This close, he could hear the wind singing in the struts that were pulled tight like piano wire between the girder-legs of the water tower. It sounded electric and dangerous.

"Yee-hah," Donny shouted. The rain had started again in a stinging drizzle and it ran down Donny's face like tears. "Leave your shit there and come on, you big pussy," he yelled, "we can't get no fucking wetter." He ran to the chain-link gate and jabbed the toes of his tennis shoes into the diamond-shaped spaces between the links and started climbing. Fisher dropped his bag and ducked under the barbed wire. He ran and leapt at the fence, snagging his fingers into it near the top. He climbed frantically and beat Donny over, dropping down onto the cinders underneath the looming bulk of the tower. The ladder to the top was made of steel hoops welded to the metal of the leg so that a climber, ascending inside the hoops, would be protected from a fall. It ended about ten or twelve feet from the ground.

"Have you ever been up one of them?" Fisher shouted.

"Sure," Donny yelled back, "plenty." He put one hand to the leg's steel as if to test it.

Goddamned liar, Fisher thought, but he didn't say it. Donny reached up and grasped either side of the leg just above his head and started to shinny up it. Thunder rumbled in the distance and Fisher thought again about the lightning. The metal of the leg was painted a dirty-looking white but big chips of the paint had flaked off and its surface was rough with dark, reddish patches of rust from which long streaks of stained red flowed. Fisher touched it and the color came off on his hand. He looked up at Donny climbing steadily away, the gray-white of his tennis shoes rising against the larger white bulk of the tank. Then Fisher hugged himself tight to the wet slickness of the leg and started climbing. The rusty roughness of the metal gave plenty of purchase and he climbed quickly despite the rain. Leaves and bits of grass blew by in a gust that howled through the guy wires and a bit of straw caught in the corner of his mouth. He pushed at it with his tongue and blew it out. The rain ran down his face and into his eyes, smelling salty and dead.

He reached the first rung and pulled himself up through the hoop. The painted iron of the hoop was slicker than the leg had been, and he almost lost his grip. He grasped and held tight to it and struggled up through the close, open-mouthed O of its circle. Once he got his feet up onto the first rung, the rest was easy, so long as he was careful not to slip.

By the time he reached the catwalk, he could feel the height without looking, its vertiginous pull like a weight down in his bowels. He pulled himself up, lying on his belly on the stretched steel of the catwalk's floor. Through the little diamond-shaped holes he could see the cinder lot far below, gray and wet and flat, and the fence with its frame of flat green. He pulled himself up to his knees, holding fast onto the catwalk's top rail. Donny was nowhere in sight. He looked out and he could see a road and a town beyond it and the stolid hunter green of woods beyond them. He stood up. The catwalk was narrow enough that he could press himself against the solid wall of the tank and still hold on to the rail. The tank felt comfortingly solid, though beneath his feet the steel mesh seemed in contrast insubstantial, filled with the perilous consequence of height, with the quavering potential for falling, for giving way. He edged carefully along, moving around the tank, looking for Donny. The wind pushed harder, needle-sharp in his right ear, trying to push its way through.

Donny was only twenty or thirty feet farther along the catwalk. He was looking out, into the storm, holding the top rail with both hands. He looked unsteady but he didn't look scared.

"It doesn't look much different," Donny shouted. "It all looks meaner'n hell, don't it?"

Fisher had thought he might see something that looked like the double-winged swirl they used on TV to show hurricanes on the maps. Or maybe the twisting, gray-black sphincter of the eye, hovering over the horizon like a whirlpool suspended over an inverted drain. It all looked the same, though, gray and heavy and blank.

Something dark and about the size of an apple blew suddenly past Fisher's head and thumped against the side of the tank, then dropped away past the catwalk to the cinders below. "Jesus!" Fisher yelled.

"What?" Donny turned his head and looked at Fisher with one eye.

"Something almost hit me. A bird maybe. I don't know." He didn't dare lean out over the railing to look for it. "I think it was a bird. God-damn, what was a bird doing in this stuff?"

"Looking to hit an asshole on a water tower, would be my guess."

"Let's get down."

"Not yet," Donny said, "look." Fisher squinted against the wind. Something swelled in the black cloud face, a bump that thinned itself out and reached down from the sky like a tongue.

"Tornado!" Donny yelled. The word terrified Fisher. The catwalk seemed suddenly thin as spider silk and horribly exposed.

"Hoo-ya!" Donny was yelling, "Goddamn! Hoo-ya! Look at that bas-tard!" Fisher watched the tornado writhe across the horizon and felt his own excitement rise like a flush of blood through his chest and upper arms. It was glorious and obscene.

"Goddamn! Shit! Bitch!" he yelled into the rushing air. The words were beautiful and infected with power.

"Yeah!" Donny shouted. "Oh, man, yeah!" Fisher jerked with both hands against the railing as if he were trying to pull it loose. He stood on his toes and crowed. He felt terrifically alive, the terror like a tremor in his blood.

"Hoo-ya!" he yelled, and yelling it he thought, *I'm going to live forever.* It was a fact, irrefutable, buzzing in his veins like wasps, frantic as the cupped-wing terror of birds. He saw himself letting go of the rail. He saw himself standing with his face to the wind, leaning out. The whole world seemed spread out below, spinning dizzy like the storm. He fell to his knees.

"Hold on, man!" Donny yelled at him.

Fisher felt the wind lift him and push him back against the stolid body of the tank and he turned to face it, his arms spread out around its middle. It was slippery and he felt himself blown past it. He felt the air take him, soaring. The sky on the far side of the tower was black with storm.

"Stop it!" he yelled, though not at the wind. At the world, waiting there for him like the embrace of a woman, the sky flowing across its face like tears.

AMERICAN STANDARD

★   ★   ★

he truth is, Billy tells himself, this is a pretty damned stupid thing to do. But he's promised to go with Royce to the bike shop to help him bring his new motorcycle home, and a promise is a promise, even if Billy hasn't been on motorcycle in probably twenty years and the whole idea makes his nouveau-middle-class-even-though-I-don't-have-a-job-anymore sensibilities shiver with dread.

The ride out is actually pretty nice, Royce's big Harley muttering through the neighborhood streets, people looking up from yard work to watch them cruise by, Royce decked out in black leather and Billy riding on the seat behind him in his jeans and tennis shoes. They get out onto Semoran and then head south to the east-west expressway. Royce gooses the Harley onto the ramp and they ease out onto the big new highway, heading west into the city of Orlando.

Royce keeps the bike up near eighty and Billy is amazed at how precarious it feels, the white stripes between the lanes blazing by like bullets a couple of feet beyond the toe of his shoe. Royce leans into the curves and Billy tries to lean with him, just a bit, though he's afraid of throwing off Royce's balance. The bike seems to swoop into the banked curves, the speed settling into his stomach and then rising again as they come out of it and level out.

The highway is mostly empty and comfortably wide, cutting a smooth eight-lane swath into the city, lifted on thirty-foot concrete piles above old neighborhoods full of gray frame houses set among palm trees and barred-window groceries and Laundromats. After a while, Royce signals for an exit, the Harley sputtering as he downshifts off the ramp onto South Orange Blossom Trail. The Trail is bleak with pawnshops and strip joints and as they ride southward down it Billy feels a pinching unease growing between his shoulder blades. Most of the places are closed for Sunday, but a thin blond girl waves at them from her station by the door of a place that advertises dollar peep shows and for half a second he's strangely tempted. Her enticement is honest and straightforward. Value for your buck. They pass by and she waves and smiles at the cars behind them.

Royce pulls the Harley in at an angle in front of a small, brick building separated out from the others on the block. On one side is a narrow, paved parking lot with about six empty spaces. The other side is hidden behind an eight-foot chain-link fence that has been woven through with strips of lime green plastic. The storefront's display windows have been painted over with black paint, making the place look deserted. The shop is small and dim and crowded with pieces of motorcycles, frames and cylinder heads and carburetors stacked and piled on the floor and on shelves made with cinder blocks and boards. The air is thick with the smell of metal and grease. It's a good smell though, clean in the way a barnyard might smell clean. No one seems to be inside, and Royce walks through the shop and goes out a door in the back and Billy follows him into a weedy lot filled with a low-set jumble of rusting motorcycle carcasses, bikes leaning randomly against each other or lying in flat piles of two or three, hoses and wires and spotty chrome pipes sprouting out of the grass like dandelions. Royce follows a narrow path through them toward a plyboard shed set in the back of the lot.

"A lot of dead bikes," Billy says.

"Dead Jap bikes," Royce tells him. "Real motorcycles never die." He intones this last like a credo. Words to live by.

Someone sees them coming and walks down the plyboard ramp that leads to the shed's double doors. He's tall and thin and bearded and wears small, round-framed John Lennon-style glasses. He's wearing dirty jeans and no shirt. At the bottom of the ramp he turns to say something to someone back in the shed and Billy sees that his hair is caught up with rubber bands into a ponytail that hangs down to the middle of his back. He holds a hand up as they get closer and says, "Hey," to Royce. "Hey Mac," Royce says back, and shakes his hand.

They all walk up the ramp into the shed. Just inside, another man sits on the floor in front of a motorcycle, an ammeter balanced on his knee. He looks up at them as they come in but doesn't say anything. Mac says, "This is my partner, Jim," and they say hello to Jim, who says "Hi," and goes back to his work. The shed is even smaller than the shop up front, but it's well lit and less crowded. The walls are filled with tools hanging on peg-boards. A half-dozen motorcycles stand waiting, all of them bearing the same familiar blue and white BMW logo.

"BMWs," Billy says. "Yuppie motorcycles. Who would've guessed?"

"Didn't even know they made bikes, did you?" Royce says.

"Never really thought about it. But, yeah, it does seem kind of odd. I thought you biker types only rode Harleys."

"Hey, it's a new world."

"Harleys are nostalgia, man," Mac says. "Poor design, and they ride like cement mixers. Too much vibration, turn your guts into jelly. In the shop more than they're on the road, too. Harleys are like hound dogs, they like to ride in the back of a truck."

"All true," Royce says. "But Harleys got style."

"They do," Mac concedes, and Billy admires him for his fairness. They all take a moment to look at the bikes, all of which are white or black or red, chunky-looking and broad compared to Royce's Sportster. The bikes look German, solid—efficient but not beautiful. The engines seem especially ungainly, the cylinder heads jutting out at right angles from the blocks like goiters.

"You make these?" Billy asks.

"Yeah, sort of. We put 'em together from parts, mostly. We get bikes people have trashed and put together new ones from the parts. Sometimes we get a whole bike that just needs some work. But, man, German engineering, these bitches last forever. And what a ride—" He's selling them now, doing his job. He squats down next to the nearest bike and taps a finger against one of the cylinder heads.

"It's called a Boxer twin—horizontally opposed cylinders. Hums like a sewing machine on the road. Very sweet. And because they stick way out like this, they stay cool. On the Harleys the back cylinder doesn't get the wind and it burns itself up. And they can save your ass, man."

He taps it again and shakes his head. "You lay a Harley down, the pavement'll turn you into hamburger, you lay a Beemer down, and the cylinder head takes the heat. I got one in a month ago, the whole damn cylinder on one side was ripped off. Guy brought it in was walking, though. He thought it was a pretty good tradeoff."

"I'll bet. That happen much? Wrecks like that?" Billy pictures what must happen to a human leg caught between a sliding five-hundred-pound motorcycle and pavement.

"Yeah, sometimes. If you're into safe, you don't ride a bike. Half the bikes I get in here for parts, the fellow who was riding it is, like, dead. Seriously dead. Hit by a truck dead."

"Christ."

"Life's a chance, Billy boy," Royce says.

"Sure," Billy says, but he's not convinced. The risk seems abstract, but not so much that he'd want to take it. He remembers how the ride over felt, as if he were balanced along with Royce above something deadly and much too close, like standing next to the tracks as a train sped by.

Mac stands back up and puts his hands in his pockets, waiting for them. Royce rubs the back of his neck, then, looking around the shed. "Well," he says, and looks back at Mac. "I thought I'd like to look at that R90 again, maybe see how she rides."

"I figured," Mac says. He leads them to the back of the shed and pulls a tarp off of a motorcycle. The bike sits square on its kickstand, the frame and tank a glossy enamel black. Billy notes that it has black panniers that look like suitcases strapped on either side of the rear wheel. Royce is looking to move up, he thinks. Royce taps at the gas tank with a fingertip.

"New tank?"

"Yeah. Couldn't save the old one, it was just too damned bunged up. Fucking shame what they did to this bike, man. I been working on this bitch for a month. She's good now, though, she'll do right by you."

"Good," Royce says. He's kneeling down, looking at one of the carburetors. "New carbs, too."

"I put Dell'Ortos back on her, took off the aftermarket pieces of shit she had. Good carbs, man. They'll squirt gas clear across a room. I could put Bings on her if you want. Not so much volume, but they're a little easier to neglect. You know, if maintenance isn't your thing."

"No, I like the Dell'Ortos," Royce says without looking up. "Frame looks good. Billy, you wouldn't believe what this bike's been through, to look this good."

"Yeah?"

"It's a story."

Mac nods. "Some yahoos smashed her up good trying to get some insurance. Rented themselves a U-Haul trailer and got one of those cargo-insurance policies, then took the damn thing with the bike in it out someplace in the boons and took turns tossing the bike out of the trailer while they're going down the road. They'd throw it out, stop, load it back up, throw it out again. You know, for a total loss. Fucked her up good. Then they make the claim, and the insurance guy says, 'hey sorry, it covers every damned thing you load into the trailer, except motor vehicles, read subparagraph so-and-so, man.' So they got shit. And one fucked-up motorcycle."

"Sounds like a bright bunch."

"Oh, yeah. And you know, the bike's got history, too, and they're out there heaving it onto the pavement like garbage."

"What's the history?"

"Used to belong to the president of one of the local motorcycle clubs.

It was his funeral bike, the one he kept nice for when one of the club members would get killed. He got killed himself a few years back, out riding stoned and tried to jump his bike over some railroad tracks and hit a telephone pole head on."

"Ouch."

"I'd say," Royce says.

"His boys still go out every year to the cemetery and put Christmas lights and stuff on his tombstone and then drink themselves shitfaced and fall asleep in the grass. They're a good bunch, getting old now, most of them got kids and real jobs. Still bikers, though."

"It's good to have friends," Royce says, and straddles the bike. He rocks forward and takes the bike down off its kickstand and balances himself and the motorcycle with the toes of his boots.

"Take her on out, man," Mac says. "She's ready."

Royce walks the bike to the shop door and rolls it down the ramp, the brakes letting out a piping little squeal as he rolls to a stop among the rows of dead motorcycles. He turns a key and pushes a button and the black BMW turns over smoothly. He flips the throttle and lets her roar for a moment.

"Lord, lord," he says, "she sounds goddamn beautiful!"

"Go for it, man. Rock and roll." Mac gestures him out the gate and Royce toes the machine into gear and gives it gas so that it leaps a little bit as he settles into the saddle. He waves as he rides out of the gate and Billy waves back self-consciously. Then he and Mac just stand there together, watching the gate, listening to the sound of the bike's motor growing more distant until it blends into the muted traffic hum.

After a minute Mac takes a battered pack of Marlboros out of the back pocket of his jeans and lights up. He offers Billy one and Billy thinks about it and then takes it and Mac lights it for him, holding his brass Zippo up between them so Billy can lean close and draw the flame into the tobacco. The cigarette tastes pleasantly sharp and feels good in his hand. Smoking makes standing there waiting for Royce seem less uncomfortable, part of something they might have done anyway, taking a moment outside, enjoying their smokes.

He hears the whine of the BMW's engine coming back up the street, Royce punching through the gears. He downshifts into the lot and pulls up beside them, revs the engine twice, then shuts it down. His cheeks above the beard are red from riding without a helmet. He takes off his sunglasses with one hand and folds them by pressing the earpieces closed one at a time against his chest. He grins at them and his eyes are bright with pleasure.

"Not a bad ride. Not bad at all."

"So you want it?" Mac drops his cigarette in the dirt and steps on it. He looks up at Royce seriously, ready for business.

"Well, now, that sort of depends," Royce says, and sits back on the bike. He puts the sunglasses away in a pocket and Billy can see they're settling down to haggle and he loses interest. This is something between them, none of his business.

He walks around the lot while they talk, looking at the dead and gutted Hondas and Suzukis. With the reputation the Japanese have for machinery, it seems strange that the American and German bikes should outlive these.

It probably has something to do with sentiment, he decides; the BMWs and Harleys must get more care, better maintenance and such, because they mean something to the bikers who own them. The Japanese bikes are, perhaps, like the carburetors Mac offered earlier: easier to neglect.

After a while, Royce calls him back. He smiles to let Billy know he's bought the bike.

★

They ride side by side in one lane, tucked in behind a tractor-trailer rig for the first mile or two, cars nudging up behind them before accelerating past. Royce takes it up to sixty-five once they're on the interstate and they move along smoothly with the traffic. The highway is massively wide, ten lanes of seamed gray concrete ticking past underneath their tires, the five southbound lanes crowded mostly with tourists in cars or RVs with northeastern and midwestern plates, Michigan and New Jersey, mostly, it seems. They start to pass traffic, though an occasional car brushes past them going even faster. Billy worries a little about running across a cop, but Royce seems unconcerned, settling back in the Harley's saddle and putting his feet up on the front pegs.

They come up on a tan-and-white Winnebago with Michigan tags lumbering down the right lane. They move by him fairly fast in the center lane, but not quite fast enough. Without warning, the big RV begins to shift over into their lane.

Billy is about even with the Winnebago's mid-section, Royce is a little ahead of him and closer to the RV. A line of cars is passing them all on the left. There's no time to brake and Royce can't know exactly where Billy is. He guns the Harley ahead, trying to get past.

Billy's watching Royce, too stunned to do anything else. Royce almost clears the RV's front bumper. The bumper catches the Harley a few inches behind Royce's hip, just a tap. The motorcycle bucks and swerves and he's certain Royce is going down, and that he'll plow into him as he drops.

Billy brakes hard and feels the back wheel lock up and start to skid. The pale aluminum side of the Winnebago looms up next to him, then recedes.

A dark shape whips by him to the left—a car. He's as certain that another car looms behind him as he can be and his whole body tenses for the blow. He's losing control of the skid, the rear end of the BMW starting to pitch to the right. His foot comes convulsively up off the brake pedal on its own; he'd forgotten the handgrip brake for the front wheel entirely.

The bike fishtails for an instant then straightens up. Ahead, the Winnebago has moved back into the right lane but keeps going. He can't see Royce and he thinks he's fallen and behind him somehow but he doesn't dare look. He brakes again, but not hard, and edges the bike across the right lane onto the paved shoulder.

Only when he's on the grass beyond and completely stopped does he look again for Royce. He doesn't see him. He gets off of the bike and lays it down on its side in the grass, the jutting cylinder head keeping it semi-upright. His hands are shaking with adrenaline and he feels disoriented and lost. Cars rush by, oblivious. A tractor-trailer roars past blowing its horn and the wind it makes buffets him, full of stinging grit like a fistful of sand.

He sees Royce then, up ahead, still on the Harley and riding slowly up the shoulder toward him. Billy pulls his helmet off and just stares at him. The man seems whole, impossibly saved. The Harley looks untouched. He rides up beside Billy and stops, taking his sunglasses off. He looks concerned for Billy, but not particularly shaken.

"Hey, bud," he shouts over the traffic noise.

"Jesus Christ, Royce, I thought you were dead."

He puts the Harley's kickstand down and pulls his helmet off. "I thought so, too, for a minute. The bastard almost got me. I got a look at him, a scared-shitless old Yankee. He just kept on trucking, probably thought I'd whip his ass or something if he stopped."

"Or sue him blind."

"Maybe so."

Billy doesn't know what to say then. He's relieved and angry and still not quite taking it all in. "You're OK, then?"

"Hell, yes." He reaches back to finger a spot behind the Harley's saddle. "He dinged the chrome a bit's all. If he'd pushed me a little harder, I probably would have lost it, though. Dumbass just didn't see us. Wasn't looking for us."

"Goddamn," Billy says. He rubs his forehead with the heel of his hand and closes his eyes for a moment. A tremor runs through his forearms and he feels a little sick.

"Shook up some?"

"You could say that."

"You must have handled yourself all right. You didn't crack the bike up. You didn't get run over."

"Yeah, that's a fact." He looks back at the BMW, lying in the grass. Another truck blows by, blasting them with grit. Royce turns his head away from it, then looks back at Billy.

"There's a rest area about a half-mile down. Why don't we motor on down to it and take a breather? Do us both some good."

He walks back to the bike. The BMW is heavier than it looks and he has to struggle with it to get it upright again, but he manages. He sits on the saddle and starts it. He takes a few deep breaths and pulls the helmet on. Royce circles the Harley around, cutting a swath through the grass and sandspurs. Billy finds it surprisingly easy to follow him: just put the bike in gear and give it gas. A moment later they're both on the highway again. Royce pushes it up to the speed limit and Billy stays with him. It's not so bad, he tells himself. He watches the cars they pass or that pass them.

People look up from their cars or from the concrete picnic tables when they ride into the rest area. They look like rough trade, he supposes, a miniature gang of two. He finds himself looking for the Winnebago in the line of parked RVs, which is silly. The guy who was driving it is probably pushing it down the highway as fast as he dares, looking for a big, snowbird-crowded KOA to hide in.

They park the bikes near an empty picnic table and Royce digs around in his saddlebags and brings out two towel-wrapped bottles of beer. They sit at the table and drink the beer, Royce spraddle-legged on one of the benches, Billy sitting on the concrete top. The beer is wonderfully good, still somewhat cold, a little bitter. There's still a tremor in his hands, but he feels better. Royce looks at his boots and doesn't drink much.

"It didn't faze you much, did it?" Billy asks him finally.

He looks at his beer, then up at Billy. "Buddy, I thought I was gonna crap in my pants. I thought that shit-for-brains Yankee in his rolling condo had killed me, sure as shit. But, man, it's happened before. It'll probably happen again. For most those folks—" He gestures at the picnickers nearby with his beer bottle "—motorcycles are invisible. Or worse, they just don't count. They don't look for us, they don't take us seriously on the road. It's like they know we can't hurt them, that whatever happens, the guy on the bike is going to lose."

"People," Billy proclaims, "are shit."

Royce shrugs. "Some are, some aren't."

"What would you have done if you'd caught up with that guy?"

"Hell, I don't know. Nothing, probably. He didn't mean to be an ass-hole, I guess. Probably busy griping at his old lady or daydreaming about his IRA, just not paying attention. Whatever. I made it. You made it. Life goes on."

Billy shakes his head. "Hell, we're talking death, Royce. Permanent and forever."

He shrugs again, drinks his beer. They sit for a while without saying anything, watching the traffic. Billy finishes his beer and tosses the bottle into the waste can chained next to the table. It clangs and rattles and the picnickers look up again disapprovingly.

Royce hands him his helmet. They mount up and start the bikes. He revs up the BMW and lets her make some noise. From the picnic tables, people shoot them annoyed looks. One woman, red-haired and heavy-set, stands up from her table, hands on her hips, and gives them an evil glare. I hope it really pisses you off, Billy wants to say to her. I hope it spoils your fried chicken and your iced tea and makes you wonder what this world's coming to. I hope you get back into your damned RV and stew over it, riding around from rest stop to rest stop buried in the smells of hair spray and baby shit and auto exhaust. I hope you open your eyes some day and look at your fat-assed husband and your ignorant, snot-faced kids and see what a fucking waste of a life you are. The beer rises in his throat, sour and acid. He puts the bike into gear and they roar down the on-ramp to the highway.

*

Later, after he gets back home, Billy thinks once again about heading over to the unemployment office to check the job board, but he can't work up any enthusiasm for it. He could run by the college, he tells himself, see about some classes maybe. Better a student than a bum. He thinks about the eighteen-year-olds that crowd the campus and feels a little desperate, though, a little left behind. Thirty-five isn't old, but it's starting to feel it. In his mind's eye, the city seems hot and hard, waver-ing on the horizon westward along the highway.

He wanders on over to Royce's, takes a couple of beers. Royce is home as usual, invites him in. Royce is still wearing his black leather motorcycle pants but he's not wearing a shirt and his skin, Billy notices, is thick with tattoos. They sit on Royce's couch and drink for a while without saying much.

Then Royce closes one eye, cocks his head and looks at Billy and says, "Hey, you think you might be interested in making a little money?"

What's this? Billy thinks. He has a fair idea of how Royce makes a living. "Nah, I don't think so," he says, but even as he's saying it, he's thinking, *well, why the hell not?* Shit, son, he tells himself, what exactly do you think you have to lose? Your self-respect? Your standing in the community? What? Freedom maybe. Prison would be one shitty damned way to spend a few years.

"'Cause it's like this, I've got a job coming up pretty quick here."

"Yeah? Doing what."

"Moving a little grass is all. From here to there. Courier stuff."

"Oh, man," Billy says, and he's thinking to himself, you're going to do this, aren't you, Billy boy? "What are we talking about, exactly?"

"Nothing much. A trip to Gainesville, drop something off, then up to Tallahassee, drop the rest off, come home. We'd pick up tomorrow evening on the bikes, you take the Beemer, then we run on up, be in Gainesville by midnight or so. We stay a night in Gainesville, or ride on up to Tallahassee if you feel cocky, whatever you want. After Tallahassee, we come home."

"God, that sounds easy."

"It is easy. That's the point. We're on bikes, so we're mobile as hell. Anything looks hinky, we just give the dope the old American Standard and light out."

"American Standard?"

"You know, like the toilets. It's a brand name, American Standard. Just dump it and go. No sweat."

"Sure," Billy says, "OK. But what the hell do you want me along for?" Royce grins at him. "Because you're just so damned pretty," he says, "what do you think?"

Billy smiles back. "Yeah, right. Seriously."

"Seriously?" Royce holds up a hand and counts on his fingers. "I could use the company. It's easier and less conspicuous on two bikes to carry this much shit. Two bikes is better on the highway because you fill the lane and people don't think they can just slide in right on top of you. And man, you look like you could use it. You get out of the house, you make some cash, life is good. What other reason do you need?"

Billy nods, thinking about it. "What the hell," he finally says. It's that simple. Not a decision, really, an acquiescence. He feels carried along. He thinks about the money and feels a hopeful spark of greed light itself in his heart.

Royce leans back again. "Cool," he says.

★

Just as Royce has promised, they reach Gainesville a little before midnight. There's still quite a bit of traffic as they ride through town, college kids mostly, Billy figures. Gainesville is a college town, built around the University of Florida, and it's lousy with students. Customers, Billy supposes, for whomever Royce is bringing the dope in for.

They ride through a stretch of town that seems to be all giant apartment complexes with names like Spring Meadows and The Cedars and keep going to where the streetlights start to be farther apart and the streets get narrower and less maintained. Royce takes them through a series of residential streets, small, older, frame houses, then more apartments, smaller buildings, concrete block, shabbier than Billy thinks students would be willing to live in. Royce pulls into the parking lot beside one, puts the kickstand down and kills the Harley's engine.

"We have arrived," he says. He takes off the Harley's saddlebags, walks over to Billy and opens the BMW's panniers and takes out two paper grocery bags.

Billy stands back from the bike, stretches and rubs the stiff muscles in his back. "You want me to come with you?"

"Not this time, partner. Just hang out here. Shouldn't take long."

Billy looks around at the parking lot. There are some kids sitting on a car hood at the other end, three of them, none older than thirteen or so,

49

he guesses. Maybe fourteen. He tries not to let the fact that the kids are black make him uneasy but it does. "Should I be worried?"

"Absolutely not. I'll be in and out in a heartbeat." He looks at Billy, looks away, looks back again like he can't quite decide to say what he's thinking of saying, then he says, "I suppose I can leave you my pistol if that'll make you feel better." He reaches a hand around under his jacket to the small of his back.

"No. Hell no. It's not a problem."

"There you go. Don't sweat it. Back in a flash." He walks toward the building's single back entrance, opens the door, waves once to Billy, and goes inside. Billy watches the door swing closed and tries not to think about what's going on, what he's doing in this town, in this parking lot. Not much of a criminal, you aren't, he tells himself. No stones for this kind of thing, no stomach for risk. Which brings up the question, he thinks, of why the fuck am I here? But he knows the answer to that. He's here because Royce is here. He's here because of the money, and because a strange sort of momentum has taken hold to move him along, and the movement feels good whatever direction it takes because anything is better than the inertia of just sitting and waiting.

He sits on the bike, puts the key back in the ignition so he can start it quick if he needs to. Then he rocks the bike down off the kickstand and walks it back so he can turn it and back it up against the fence. He thinks about doing the same for Royce's bike, but he decides against it. That would look a little too anxious, a little too yellow. He leaves the kickstand up, balancing himself and the bike with his toes.

He waits. The kids at the far end of the lot watch him and he's watching them while trying to look as if he isn't. So he doesn't see the man in the dirty green army fatigue jacket coming until the guy looms next to him. Billy jumps and leans away and the bike tilts and he has to struggle to keep it upright. He gets the bike steadied and twists around to face the guy, his heart pounding in his chest so hard it's painful. The man just stands there without saying anything and there's just enough light that Billy can see his face, black, very dark, broad nostrils outlined with what look like rings of gold dust. They stare at each other for a long moment.

"That just Goldie," someone says. Billy glances away long enough to see that one of the kids has come about halfway across the lot and is standing watching them. "He wacked, man. He sniff paint." The gold dust, Billy realizes, is gold paint caked in circles where the guy has been inhaling the stuff.

"What do you want?" he asks Goldie. Goldie doesn't move or say a word, he just stares at Billy.

"Give 'im a dollar," the boy suggests.

Billy thinks about it, reaches for his wallet, thinks better of that, thinks it might be better if he keeps his wallet out of sight, and digs instead for the change in his pants pocket. He comes up with a quarter and some dimes and offers them. Goldie keeps on staring for a moment, then slowly holds his hand out. Billy drops the change into his palm. Goldie looks down at the money, closes his hand. He walks off out of the lot and into the street.

"Thanks, man," Billy says to the boy.

"Yeah." The kid goes back to his friends and climbs up on the car.

"Shit," Billy says under his breath. He watches the door for Royce and tries not to think, tapping his fingers against the BMW's gas tank.

The door opens and Billy tenses, squints against the light to see who it is, but it's just Royce, carrying his saddlebags. Royce jogs over and it alarms Billy that he seems to be in a hurry.

"What is it?" he asks as Royce comes up.

"Nothing," Royce says. "Think fast," he says, and he tosses something at Billy. Billy grabs and catches it. It's a packet of money, crisp bills in a bank's currency band.

"What's this?"

"Your half of the profits," Royce says. He lifts the Harley's saddle and secures the saddlebags. "Put it in your pocket and crank her up. We need to get on out of here."

"Why?"

"Explain later," Royce says. He hops onto the Harley and starts it and

Billy follows suit, cranking the BMW and waiting for Royce to push the Harley back. He puts the money into the inside pocket of his jacket. Then he puts the bike into gear and follows Royce out of the lot.

They ride back the way they came, but faster, and Billy worries at what's gotten Royce into a hurry. He feels a crawling sensation between his shoulder blades and he glances back a couple of times to see if anybody's following, but the street behind them is deserted. He's a little surprised when Royce signals for a turn into a gas station. Royce rolls up the pumps, puts his kickstand down. Billy stops on the opposite side of the same pump and pulls his helmet off.

"What's up?" he asks.

"Gas. What, you think these things run on love and promises?"

"Come on, Royce."

"Not a thing," he says. He looks at Billy and then back the way they've come. "I dunno. Everything went fine, the money was right. I just felt a little nervous coming out. I don't know why. You get these intuitions, you know, and then you find out they aren't for shit and you feel stupid."

"You thought something was going to happen."

"Nah. Just nervous 'cause your rookie ass is along." He smiles to let Billy know he's kidding. "Let's get some fuel and get on down the road."

Billy's glad he doesn't seem interested in staying the night. Royce's nervousness has him feeling spooked. The whole town feels heavy with something, some potentiality. He looks at his watch and it's nearly one in the morning. Long night in the saddle, but at least they'll be out of Gainesville.

Royce pays for the gas and they roll out of the station toward the highway. They come up to a traffic light and Billy pulls the clutch in, but the light changes to green before he can brake. He lets the clutch out again but he then he sees movement out of the corner of his eye and hesitates, pulling it back in so that Royce surges ahead. Billy sees a car come blowing out of the darkness of the side street and for an instant he thinks it's slowing down for the light and then he knows that it isn't.

Royce is in the intersection and Billy sees him wrench the throttle open and the Harley leaps forward.

But it's too late and Billy realizes he's known it's too late since he saw the first motion of the car like a flicker in the near distance. Something like a weight inside his heart seems to hold him motionless. He doesn't even think to put on the BMW's brakes until the car is by him. The car swerves and in the cold, single moment of impact Royce flies free of the Harley and tumbles across the pavement.

Billy sees this, though there is nothing about it he can believe is real. He jams convulsively on the foot brake and before he can think the rear of the bike starts to pitch out and the tire slips out from under. The bike goes down and slides, sparks showering from the cylinder head as it grinds across the pavement. He feels a sudden shock of pain in his knee as it hits the road and without thinking he puts his hand down and it's snatched backwards. The bike hits something solid, the curb, maybe, and he's pitched away hard, rolling.

Then he's lying on his back. Everything is still.

He can smell a burnt odor. And grass, as if someone has mown a yard nearby. The pain in his leg is incredible, but he can also feel his hand and forearm throbbing. Something is wrong there. He tries to get his helmet off, but his right hand isn't working right and it hurts like hell to try to work the strap. He finally gets it loose with his left and pitches the thing away from him.

Then he tries to get up and the pain is like an ice pick through his kneecap. He does it anyway, levers himself up on one knee and then, with a mighty effort, up on his feet so most of his weight is on the un-hurt leg. He hops to where Royce is lying on his side on the pavement and goes down on his one good knee beside him. Royce isn't moving and there's blood on his legs and his helmet is split, a neat seam up one side like a crack in an eggshell. Billy thinks to take the helmet off, and then thinks that he doesn't dare. He hardly even knows how to touch Royce. He remembers all the movies he's seen with people looking for a pulse but he's unsure how to do that or even if he should. His hands are

53

shaking and he feels faint and nauseated. He pushes the visor up, gently, so gently, and Royce's face is pale and bloody beneath it, his eyes closed, his mouth open and gaping.

Then somebody is there. Billy looks up and there's a teenager, a boy of maybe seventeen standing over him, a college kid. Billy can see the car that hit Royce beyond him, its door open, and he thinks about Royce's money and he looks at the boy and expects violence, feels his muscles tense for it. But the kid is crying and slobbering and Billy realizes he's drunk.

"Are you OK?" the kid moans. He sways over them.

"Not me," Billy says, "not me, you asshole."

"Oh, god. Oh, Jesus." He turns, stumbles away a few feet and vomits.

Billy struggles to stand and looks wildly around. He sees that Royce's saddlebags have split open. There's dope and money spread across the pavement, and some of the cash is fluttering in the breeze like leaves. He's disoriented and it takes him a moment to find the gas station. He starts hopping toward it, putting just enough weight on his injured leg to move, just enough to feel as if it's trying to tear loose with every step he takes. The woman who sits in the booth at the station is standing outside of it looking down the road at the accident.

"Call an ambulance," Billy shouts at her. He's almost crying with the shock and frustration. "Call a fucking ambulance."

She ducks back into her booth and he stops, standing in the middle of the road. He closes his eyes and stands there, it seems like only a few moments, but when he opens his eyes he can suddenly hear sirens. The grief in their rising wail is so perfect that he can hardly face it, but he does. He watches them come. In the distance, red and blue lights begin to flicker and twist like bright little demons setting fires in the trees, burning back the darkness that does its best to fill the southern night.

He hobbles back, and because he can't think of anything else to do, he goes to the BMW and levers it up, though the pain in his leg is fierce. The bike starts at the first touch of the button. Good honest German engineering. He balances the bike and tries to work his bad leg up across the saddle. The drunk kid watches him stupidly without saying anything. A couple of cars have stopped, and people are gaping. Money blows off under the cars in a parking lot. When Billy is on the bike, he guns the throttle and the motorcycle bolts out into the unlit stretch of pavement across the intersection, and it's only then that he realizes the headlight is broken. He keeps going anyway, hurtling into the night, the BMW humming faithful as a lover. He can feel the money Royce gave him pressing against his chest, a hot promise. The road opens up before him, blind and wild and running away forever through the darkness. He twists the throttle open as wide as it will go and flies out to meet it.

MOVING MAN

★   ★   ★

After the fourth ring, the machine in the living room picked up. It was a student, she had heard he helped students move their stuff from one apartment to the next, and she wanted her things moved. He decided he'd call her back later. He turned the TV on and settled into the couch. He fell asleep in the middle of *The Young and the Restless*. Victor was romancing Jack's wife while Jack and Brad plotted to steal Newman Industries from under Victor's preoccupied nose. Everyone vigorously screwing everyone else. Art, as usual, he thought, imitating life.

When he woke, the single eye of the machine's red call light was blinking at him from the dark living room. He thought about the seven dollars in ones he had in his wallet and dialed. A man's voice answered. He asked for Catherine, and the voice told him to hang on a minute.

When she came to the phone, her voice sounded strange and strained. He thought, maybe she's been crying, or yelling, or both.

"What?" she said.

"I'm the guy you called about moving. You called this morning some time."

"I called *hours* ago."

56

"Yeah," he said. "I've been busy. Lots of people need help moving."

She was quiet for a long moment. He heard a door slam on the other end of the line. It was a distant sort of sound, made thin by the wire. "Yes. Well. Could you come get my stuff for me? Today?"

He checked his watch. It was almost four. "What time did you have in mind?"

"This morning's when I had in mind."

He resisted the impulse to drop the handset back on the hook. "Look, do you want my help or what? I can be there in a half-hour or so. You're near the campus?"

"Yes." She gave him directions. "Listen," she said, "I'd really appreciate it if you'd come over here now. I need to get out of here." She surprised him then by sobbing, a choked and heartbroken sound.

"OK," he told her. "I'll be there shortly."

"OK." She hung up.

He went outside to the truck and loaded his tarps and the dolly into the bed. The afternoon air was heavy with the smells of hot tar and cut grass. All over the city, cars were pulling into driveways. Long day at the office, daddy's coming home.

He started the truck and backed it out. As he pulled away, he saw his neighbor's wife watching from their front door. She was ugly, as usual, and wearing the usual grungy housedress. He waved to her because he knew she was scared of him and she disappeared like a ghost back into the dimness inside.

"You ought to be scared," he said out loud. He made a face at her closed door. "Crazy man," he said.

★

He found the student's apartment more quickly than he had thought he would. She was sitting on the grass in front of her building on a small, neat pile of her belongings, crying hard. His first thought was that it was ungodly hot to be sitting in the sun crying.

She heard the pickup's brakes squeal and looked up. Her face was red and streaked with tears and she was very pretty and very sad. He stopped the truck and got out. She watched him coming around the truck, her hands crossed across her stomach.

He stood there in front of her, feeling lame and clumsy. After a minute she dragged a pink towel out of a shopping bag and mopped her face. He looked away into the distance over her head. "You're Catherine."

She nodded. "Yeah. That's right."

"Is there anything else in the apartment?"

"My desk," she said. He could hardly hear her. She had cried her voice out. "First room to the left, inside the door. Upstairs, 3C."

He yanked the dolly out of the truck's bed and climbed the stairs that ran up the side of the building. The steps were cheap welded iron, the treads filled with beige concrete, and they creaked under his weight. He opened the door of 3C and went in, pushing through the blast of cold air being sucked out the door by the heat.

A blond-haired boy of maybe nineteen or twenty was sprawled across a couch, watching MTV on a big, expensive-looking Sony.

"Her shit's already outside," the boy said.

"She wanted me to get the desk."

He shrugged. "Fine by me. I just want the crazy bitch out."

"OK."

"You better make sure she pays your ass in advance, you want some advice. I kid you not, that bitch is nuts."

He rolled the dolly in and opened the first door to the right. The desk was against the near wall, a compact rolltop made of some dark reddish wood, mahogany or cherry. The only other object in the room was an unmade waterbed. He tilted the desk a bit and slipped the dolly's blade underneath, then eased the weight back until it was balanced on the wheels. He worked the desk out the door, the boy watching him without moving. When he had it out on the landing, the kid got up and closed the door. He bumped the dolly down the steps and rolled it across the grass to the truck.

The girl was standing by the truck, looking dubiously into the bed.

"It's awfully rusty in there, isn't it?"

"That's what the tarps are for. Your stuff'll be fine, if nothing spontaneously combusts." The sweat from his forehead was running into his eyes and he used the sleeve of his T-shirt to wipe at it. "Hot," he said.

"What did he say?" she asked. Her voice got thin and painful again.

"The guy upstairs?"

"Yes."

"Not much. Just that your stuff was already out."

"Bastard," she said, "skinny prick."

He didn't know what to say to that. He spread one of the tarps, tilted the desk back on the dolly and got one corner up on the tailgate, then got under it with his shoulder and heaved it into the bed, sliding it across the tarp until it nudged tight against the cab. Then he started loading the rest of her things, most of it in paper grocery sacks, most of it clothes and CDs and some kitchen stuff.

She lit a cigarette and watched. Her hands were shaking, and after a minute she knelt down and put the cigarette out in the grass, then stood with her arms crossed, staring at the curb. He glanced at her every once in a while as he worked. Twice she caught him at it and the second time she rolled her eyes.

"I'd think you'd have seen plenty of upset women, doing what you do."

"Well, not as many as that, I guess. A few."

"Well, don't look at me. I feel like shit."

"You look fine. Great, in fact."

She grimaced at him and rolled her eyes again. "Oh, God, that's what I need. Handyman pity." She walked to the front of the truck and leaned against the fender, looking away. After a minute she started crying again and hid her face in the pink towel.

He left her alone and arranged the last few bags in the truck, then tied a second tarp down over everything so nothing would blow out. When he was finished, he walked around to the driver's side and climbed into the cab. He had to tap on the windshield with a knuckle to get her attention.

"You coming?"

She looked down at him through the glass, then yanked irritably at the door handle. She was wearing shorts and a tank top, but she got into the truck as if she were wearing a skirt, sitting first, then swinging her legs gracefully in, her knees together. Her feet were bare. She caught him looking again.

"My feet swell when I'm unhappy."

"Sorry."

"Not your problem."

"Nope." He put the truck into gear. "Where to?"

She didn't answer and for a minute he had the panicky feeling that she had nowhere to go and that he'd have to deal with it. He saw her suddenly as one of those screwed up little coeds, the ones who went wild the moment they were away from home and drank themselves stupid on the weekends and screwed a load of fraternity types and ended up broken and someday having to explain to daddy or to a husband about the herpes or the abortions.

Finally, she sighed to herself and folded the pink towel in her lap. "Park Avenue. Over in Winter Park."

He let up on the brake and turned the truck around. Traffic had started to ease some, and he made good time until they reached the big intersection at Semoran, where things piled up again. She asked him if he cared if she smoked, he said no, and she rolled down her window and lit a Marlboro with a blocky-looking brass Zippo. When she had the cigarette lit, she looked at the lighter and snorted.

"Funny lighter?" he asked.

"Stolen lighter. Ex-boyfriend's I-used-to-be-a-Marine lighter. 'Semper Fi' engraved on it. 'Always Faithful,' my ass."

"That blond kid was a Marine?" He was surprised. The kid had looked pretty much like your average college-aged deadhead.

"Kid? Don't judge a book by its cover. That blond kid's a mean son of a bitch going to college on some GI thing. Black belt in karate, too. A real ass kicker. A real ass*hole*."

"Sounds like a winner."

"What the fuck do you know?" She was angry again.

"Not a damned thing. I'm just a handyman."

She was quiet again for a while. They made it to the intersection as the light turned yellow and he gunned it on through. Somebody blew a horn.

"I'm sorry I said that," she told him. "What's your name?"

Some atavistic impulse made him want to lie. He almost told her his name was John.

"Dave," he said.

"Dave. Like in David."

"Yup."

"Cool." She said the word the way a character he'd seen on a TV commercial did, as a wiseassed little bark. He looked at her and she smiled just a bit, and he realized she was even prettier than he had thought, the kind of smooth, magazine pretty that was very scary when you were right next to it. Her face was still red and streaked, and he felt suddenly uneasy. When he looked back at her again, she had rolled the towel up and was twisting it in knots around her hand.

"Winter Park. Pretty ritzy neighborhood. You're moving back in with your parents?"

"My parents live in Cambridge. In Massachusetts."

"Oh. Long drive to school. From Winter Park, I mean."

"I quit two semesters back."

"Oh."

That was the end of the conversation for a while. He concentrated on the traffic and she smoked her cigarette, blowing the smoke out the window. Just outside of Winter Park she sat up.

"That's a pretty little lake," she said, pointing. Water sparkled off behind the businesses that lined the road.

"That's not a lake, really," he told her. "Or at least it wasn't a few years back. Twelve or thirteen years ago that was a couple of houses and a Porsche dealership."

"Yeah? What do you mean?"

"Sinkhole. Started in somebody's backyard and then just got wider and wider and deeper and deeper until things started to disappear, like houses and sixty thousand dollar German sportscars. They got a couple of the cars out with helicopters. Then the hole filled up with rain. The houses and the rest of the Porsches are still down there, under the water somewhere."

"Jesus. How did that happen?"

"The sinkhole? They're everywhere around here, just waiting to open up. All of this under us is limestone that's just rotten through with caves, really big ones, sometimes. The caves are usually filled up with water, but there's so damned many people living here now, the water table gets low and the caves' roofs collapse. Bingo, sinkhole. One of them opened up not long ago in the middle of a highway, about three in the morning, and people just drove right into it in the dark, sixty feet down. Splash."

"Cool," she said, and this time he could tell that she meant it.

"Yeah, unless you're sleeping in that house or driving that car."

"Even then," she said.

*

He turned onto Park behind a tractor-trailer rig and followed it down the narrow street as it wound through the old part of Winter Park. Oak trees leaned in close above the road, and a steady shower of leaves and twigs pelted the pickup's windshield as the semi's trailer brushed through the canopy overhead.

"Over there," she said, pointing at a pet store in the middle of a block.

"Wings and Things," he read off of the door. "Sounds like a fried chicken joint."

"The apartment's on top. Pull around behind."

He went on to the end of the block and took a left, then pulled into the alley that ran behind the pet shop. He parked in front of a door that opened out beside a dumpster. A woman about his age but dressed younger, in day-glo colors, with black, straight hair cut boy-short, stood in the door. She waved at them, palm out, like she was polishing glass.

"Kitty!" she said. "I saw you go by out front with the stuff in the truck and I figured it might be you."

Catherine shoved the truck door open and stepped out. "Hi," she said, and they hugged each other. Catherine—Kitty, now—gestured toward him. "That's Dave. He's helping me move."

"Hi, Dave. I'm Leni." She waved again.

He waved back and climbed out of the pickup. He loosened the ropes holding the tarp and grabbed a couple of bags. Leni held the door open for him and Kitty stood aside. Inside, there was a hallway leading to the front and a narrow carpeted staircase to the left. He started up the stairs.

The door at the top was open and he walked on in.

"Where should I put all this?" he called back. Leni and Kitty were climbing the stairs slowly, talking. Leni looked up at him.

"We're just talking about that. Put it in the living room for now."

"I'd forgotten you don't have any AC," Kitty said.

"Nope. No AC. Just a fan. But it's not bad when you get used to it. All the oaks on the street keep the building shaded. I was thinking I might get a couple of little window jobs for the bedrooms, for sleeping."

"Yeah. OK."

"We're ready to settle in, then," Leni said to him.

"Good."

A bell tinkled somewhere downstairs. "Back in a sec," Leni said, then disappeared back down the stairs. Kitty looked as if she were going to cry again.

"Not what you expected?" Dave asked.

"It's what I can afford, which is about nothing. Leni's nice to let me stay here." She passed a hand across her forehead.

"Leni seems all right."

"Yeah," she said, "yeah." She sat glumly on the couch.

"I'll get your things."

"Yeah." She put her head down on the arm of the couch and closed her eyes. He noticed how pleasantly musty the room smelled, like old wood and dust. A sprawling oriental carpet covered the wooden floor to within a foot or so of the walls. It was spotted here and there with bird droppings.

Leni was back by the time he got around to the desk. She helped keep it steady on the dolly while he dragged it backwards up the stairs.

"Friend of Kitty's?" Leni asked.

"Nope. I just own the truck."

"Ah." She shoved as he pulled and the dolly's wheels rose over the edge of a tread and thumped softly against the carpeted riser of the next step.

"Sell a bird?"

"No. Just a lookie-loo. Lots of folks look, not too many take anything out with them. Everybody's scared of commitment, even to a bird. That's why I need a roommate. Have to defray some overhead."

She tilted her head out from around the desk to look at him. He noticed then that her nose was pierced. She wore a tiny diamond stud in her left nostril. It looked strange and out of place on her face, like a glittery flyspeck.

"She doesn't seem really happy about the place, does she?"

"She told me it's what she can afford." He felt uncomfortable talking to a stranger about a girl he hardly knew who might well have been able to hear what was being said.

"Well, she knew it wasn't great. I told her. People don't listen." She sighed. "Lord, I sound old. Like my mother. I'm only thirty-five, you know?"

"Yeah," Dave said. He pulled and she shoved and they rose another step, then once more and the desk was on the landing. They maneuvered it through the door, then he braced the dolly with his foot and eased the desk down next to the pile of paper bags. He could see that Kitty had fallen asleep on the couch. She looked uncomfortable there, and vulnerable. The late afternoon light came through the window over her head in yellow squares, and he could see the dust in it, raining down to disappear into her hair.

"Where do you want the desk?" he asked Leni.

"Oh, I don't know," she whispered. She was looking at Kitty, too. "We'll figure it out, I guess. This is all her stuff? You're not going back for more?"

"As far as I know, this is it."

Leni sighed and shook her head. "Yeah. You don't even know her." She looked at the pile. "That's it, then?"

"Yeah, except that she hasn't paid me yet."

Leni went to the couch and gave Kitty's shoulder a little shake and she sat up, blinking.

"Whoops," she said, very quietly. "Sorry, folks."

"No problem," Leni said. "This fellow needs his money, though."

She took a deep breath. "Sure. Just a second." He watched while she found her purse and dug through it for her wallet. She counted out the money as he watched, her fingers thin and graceful, her knuckles tanned brown as hazelnuts against the green bills.

As he went, Kitty's voice followed him out. "Hey, handyman. Watch out for sinkholes," she said.

*

Three days later he drove past the storefront with the Wings and Things sign and found a parking spot not too far away in front of a frozen yogurt shop. He sat in the truck for a while, thinking, before he climbed out and fed the meter its quarter for a half-hour's parking. He thumped the meter with the palm of his hand to give himself the momentum to start walking, but when he did manage to put one foot in front of the other, he found it easier to head up Park Avenue—away from the pet shop—and so that's what he did, telling himself he'd come back down on the other side of the street so he could look into the store from a little distance.

He walked two blocks up, past the store windows filled with wood carvings and candles shaped like animals and towering, dark, antique armoires. He crossed the street at the light and walked slowly back until he was even with his truck. Then he lost his nerve, impulsively cut back across the street, and walked around to the driver's side door to get in and go home.

Just as reached for the door handle, the bell over the door of the frozen yogurt shop tinkled and Leni walked out, pushing the door with her shoulder, a cup of frozen yogurt in each hand. Dave hurried over and held the door open for her.

"Thanks," Leni said, and then, "don't I know you?"

"Yeah, sure," Dave told her. "The moving guy. Kitty's stuff."

"Oh, yeah, right. Dave, right?"

He nodded. "Yeah, and you're Leni."

"Yeah. I'm good that way, at names. You too, I guess, huh?" Someone cleared his throat behind her, and she stepped on through the door to make way. "So, Dave, what brings you back here?"

Dave put his hands in his pockets. He tried to sound casual. "Just running an errand," he said. "Thought I might get some yogurt, too."

Leni laughed. The tiny diamond in her nose sparkled. "Me, too. Business is slow, so Kitty's watching the shop while I get us some of the ol' frozen stuff."

"Yeah," Dave said, "I see."

"Well, OK," Leni said. "I'll see you." She nodded and smiled and turned away.

"Yeah," Dave said. "Nice talking to you. Hope business picks up."

"We can always hope," Leni said over her shoulder. "Hope is good."

"You bet," Dave said. He watched her walk away for a minute, then thought it might be bad if she caught him watching her. He went into the yogurt shop and the girl behind the counter looked up when the bell jingled and smiled at him. He ordered chocolate with bits of Oreo cookie mixed in and sat at a table by the window. He ate it slowly because his hands were shaking so hard the spoon clattered against the yogurt cup.

★

He'd been home an hour when the phone rang. He thought about letting the machine get it, but he was feeling down enough to talk to even a student, if that's who was calling. No one else seemed to call anymore.

"Hey, Dave," a woman's voice said. "It's Leni. With the yogurt. And the birds."

"Oh, yeah. Hi," he said. "What can I do for you?" Too strange, he was thinking. Just too strange.

"Oh, hey, well, I was thinking. You know, you seem like a really nice guy. Kitty thinks so, too. I got your number from her. I've got this dinner I'm supposed to go to for the Chamber of Commerce and all. I'm a member and all, you know, because of the store, and, well, I've got these tickets, and . . . oh, God, I can't believe I'm even doing this, you know. This really makes me look like I'm desperate or something, doesn't it?"

"I'm not following you."

"I'm, like, asking you out, Dave. I thought maybe you'd like to go to this thing with me. Free food and booze, maybe some dancing. You know? I wasn't going to go at all, but since I got the tickets, and you seemed like a really nice guy. . . ."

Well, Dave thought, now this is a development. He didn't know what to say. The dead air became loud over the phone line. "Jeez," Leni said, "I knew this was probably a really bad idea. . . ."

"No," Dave broke in. "It's OK. You just surprised me a little bit."

"OK," Leni said. More dead air. Then, "Well, what do you think? Would you like to give it a go?"

"Well, yeah, sure," Dave said. He was thinking, hell, why not? "When did you have in mind?"

"Well, I'm afraid it's tonight. Is that a problem?"

"No, I don't think so. In fact, that'd be great."

"Great," Leni said. She sighed. "Wow. This is hard, isn't it? Look, would you like me to come pick you up, or would that be just too weird?"

"Yeah, maybe," Dave said. "I'll come by and get you, I think. If that works for you."

"Yeah, great. Six?"

"Six."

"Great. Look, I better go. . . ."

"Sure," Dave said. "I'll see you tonight."

"Great," Leni said again. "Bye." And she hung up.

Dave put the phone back on the receiver. He sat down on the couch and blew out a heavy breath. "Great," he said to no one in particular.

★

Kitty came to the door when he knocked and then stood there for a long moment without saying anything, looking out at him, trying, he thought, to make him feel nervous. It felt close in the alley, in the heat and dumpster stink. She was wearing white jogging shorts and a wine-colored blouse that looked a lot like a man's polo shirt. Probably was a man's polo shirt, Dave thought, the boy marine's. An alligator sewn on above her left breast. He had to consciously control his hand to keep from reaching out to touch it, little green monster, jaws open. "Yeah," he said. "I'm looking for Leni."

"Hi. Yeah, I know. Leni had a bird problem," she said. "Come on in for a minute." She stood aside to make room and he walked past her into the dimness of the hallway. Somewhere up front in the store a parrot let out a single angry squawk.

"She had to go out to the airport. Some birds died or something, on a plane. They were being shipped, I think, like from South America or something. She had to do some paperwork, view the bodies, something like that." She wasn't looking at him much while she talked. She was looking over his shoulder into the alley. He resisted the urge to turn around and look himself.

"Ah," he said instead. She looked at him finally, and smiled just a bit, with one corner of her mouth. He took it awkwardly and smiled back, feeling foolish.

"Come on upstairs," she said. "Leni told me she'd call around six if she could get to a phone, to let us know what's going on."

"Sure." He followed her up the steps, averting his eyes monkishly from her rear end as it hovered before him. If I look, he thought, she'll turn. Halfway up, she looked back over her shoulder as if to catch him.

"How are you getting along with the birds?"

"Don't ask." She grimaced, and he thought, this is somebody's little girl, blond-haired and too damned lovely.

The phone rang with a tinny, antique buzz. Kitty looked across the couch to where an old, black rotary phone sat on a table made of cinder blocks. It rang again.

"Could you answer that?" she said. She crossed her arms. "It's probably Leni but it might not be."

The phone rang a third time. "The marine?"

"Yeah, maybe. He's called a few times. Leni told him to go fuck himself once. I think he took it personally, at least I hope he did. He's been calling back every once in a while just to keep us on our toes. I've threatened to call the cops, but he hasn't been impressed."

"Oh," he said. He went to the phone and picked up the handset just as it started to ring again.

"Hello," he said. He couldn't remember Leni's last name so he left it at that. There was silence for a long moment on the other end, then Leni's voice.

"Who's this?" she asked, very tentative.

"Dave," he told her. "The moving man."

"Oh, right. Dave." She sounded relieved. "Christ, I'm really sorry. I had a couple of cockatoos die on me. They were just going to chuck 'em and pay off the insurance, but I thought I ought to come over here, just to check it out. Who knows, they probably can't tell a dead bird from a live one. I hate this. I'm really sorry."

"Can you make it back?" He glanced at his watch.

"God, I don't think so." She sighed. "Not for a while, anyway. They make everything so complicated, these damned airlines."

"Yes, I know," he said. It was amazing to him how disappointed he felt. "Maybe some other time."

"You're pissed, aren't you? I can tell."

"No. It's all right. Really. Don't worry about it."

"Yeah, OK." She was quiet for a moment, then, "Put Kitty on the phone, will you?"

He sensed something and hesitated, then motioned to Kitty to come over. He handed her the phone. "She wants to talk to you."

"Yes?" she said into the handset, then, "Uh-huh?" and then she listened for a long minute. "Sure, bye," she finally said, and hung up the phone.

"What's up?"

"She wanted to know if I'd take you to the dinner. She feels bad."

"Listen—" he said.

"It's OK, really," she broke in. She sat down on the chair across from him. "It's not like a pity thing, or anything. Free dinner for both of us, the tickets are on the corkboard. I was wondering what the hell I was going to do with myself tonight anyway. No big deal. Just give me a few minutes to change."

"Jeez," he said. His face felt hot.

"Aw, don't fight it, moving man. It's a done deal." She smiled and stood up and walked to the bedroom, looking at him coyly over her shoulder. "Back in a flash."

He watched her go, feeling a little numb. Something frightening and delightful had happened very quickly while he watched, at the center of it but uninvolved. He slouched down in the couch's broken softness and listened with his eyes closed to water rush in a sink. The water was shut off with a squeak of old plumbing. Then it was quiet, then soft, mysterious sounds that he couldn't place but could imagine. Rustlings and soft bumps. He felt suddenly more than a little aroused. He heard flesh slap gently against something—elastic maybe—and thought he might jump out of his skin.

He heard Kitty come back into the room. He opened his eyes. She stood near him, wearing a sparkling peach-colored blouse and tight, black jeans.

"Hey, don't get too comfortable," she said. She smiled at him. "There's a dinner out there with our names on it, you know."

★

Dinner was pleasant, plain food and speeches, but she was there. Afterwards, he drove out onto the expressway and pushed the truck until they were doing eighty through the darkness, breezing past most of the cars on the road as though they were parked, the wind roaring in through the open windows. The road lifted up on its concrete pillars into the lighted city and they passed among the sparkling high-rises.

"Say," Kitty said when they were coming up to the exit for the South Orange Blossom Trail, "why don't you pull off here."

He eased the truck over into the exit lane and down the ramp. They rolled onto the Trail and out among the strip joints and pawnshops and fast-food franchises. The Trail was crowded with cars; a lot of them seemed to be full of teenagers out cruising, driving and drinking beer and trying to get up the courage to attempt to get past the ID checkers posted like sentries at the doors of the bars.

There was shouting from a strip club as they passed, and what looked like a bachelor party poured out of a long black limousine and through the bar's double doors, young guys wearing slacks and ties, eager as hounds.

He pointed them out. "Another long night of cheap thrills."

Kitty looked. "Not so cheap," she said. "But it's a guy thing, I guess. Pay good money to look at tits."

He was a little startled. "I suppose that's so. Probably not too many women paying to look at 'em."

She gave him a look that was hard to read. A little dour, a little mysterious. "Oh, you'd be surprised, old son."

"Oh, yeah?"

"Yep," she said. "Trust me on it."

He shrugged. "OK."

"Ahhh, you're too easy," she said, and reached over and gave him a shove.

"OK," he said.

"OK," she said back to him. Then she leaned over and put her hand on the side of the steering wheel and gave it a little jerk to one side so the truck yawed out of the lane, tires squealing. A van coming in the other direction dodged off away from them, blowing its horn.

"Shit!" He dragged the truck back into its lane. "What'd you do that for?"

"Relax," she said. "Just trying to liven things up."

"Well, don't do that."

She put her hand against his cheek. "OK," she said, "I won't. Maybe you should take me home."

He looked at her. She didn't seem upset. "Why?"

"Who knows?" she said.

There was something unexpected there, and he was not sure how to react to it. "I don't think I want to," he said.

She leaned close and kissed him softly under his jaw. "Sure you do," she whispered.

"Sure I do," he said.

★

Kitty unlocked the back door to Leni's place and turned to him. She took his hand and led him inside. He followed, silent and wondering why. A little suspicious, because he could think of no reason why she would want to do this. He was just Dave, after all, broke and lonely and nobody's prize. The moving man. And yet here was this girl. And yet.

Upstairs, the apartment was dark, though light from the street lamps poured in through the front window. Kitty came up to him and took both of his hands, closed her eyes and kissed him. Then she smiled at him and pushed him slowly back toward the couch where he had watched her sleeping that first day. She pushed him down so that he was sitting on the couch and kissed him again. He put his hands on her waist and started to pull her down with him but she resisted. The light from the window cut across her at an angle, oyster-gray and dim. She took a step back from him and turned around slowly, swaying her hips.

"What do you see?" she whispered.

He didn't know what to say. "It's great—"

She shook her head. "No, what do you *see?*"

"I don't know. You. I see you."

"Yeah," she said, "that's right. Me." She swung her head back and forth, her eyes closed.

"I danced for a while at one of those clubs on the Trail," she said. "Does that shock you?"

"No," he said. "Maybe some."

"That's where I met Leni." She came back close to him and kissed his forehead, rubbing her lips across his skin. He didn't reach for her this time and she moved slowly back away from him again and pirouetted

72

as gracefully as a danseuse. Eyes closed, she unbuttoned her blouse and let it drop.

"I danced for her," she said. "She paid me, and I danced." She undid her bra and dropped it, too. She leaned close to him.

"This is what I did for Leni. You like it?" she whispered. He nodded. "She liked it, too."

"OK." He didn't want to say anything else, but he did anyway. "I don't get it," he said.

"Do you have to?"

"I don't know."

"Shit," she said. She straightened and took a step back from him. "I don't need this." She stooped to pick up her blouse and he thought how hard she looked. Nobody's little girl.

"I didn't mean—"

"Hey, just screw you," she said, so casually he couldn't tell how she meant it. She dropped the blouse onto the coffee table and picked up a pack of cigarettes. She tapped one out over her knuckle, put it in her mouth and lit it with the marine's Zippo. She snapped the lighter closed and stood looking at Dave, topless and smoking. Looking tough and matter-of-fact. Waiting for him to say something.

He couldn't look at her, so he looked at the cigarette in her hand instead. Saw the cherry-spot of its end bump and flicker because, he realized, her hands were shaking. He felt huge and lethargic in the couch, unable to move.

"Well—" he began.

"Oh, brilliant," she said, "Jesus."

"Look—"

"Just shut up," she said. She dropped the cigarette on Leni's carpet and ground it out with her heel. "Just shut up, OK?"

He shut up. She stripped off her jeans and tossed them onto the table with the blouse. "Shut up, will you? That's not so much to ask." He could hear a softening in her voice and he felt absurdly hopeful all over again.

73

"No, it's not," he said.

"You're damned right," she told him.

★

Later the phone rang. Kitty stirred and looked at it, then looked to Dave. "I guess Leni put the damned thing back on the hook," she said. "Maybe you could get it?"

"Sure," he told her. "No problem." He was loath to get up, though. Kitty lay beside him on the bed, looking through the bedroom door at the phone on its table by the couch. A tattooed ring of blue flowers wound its way around her left ankle, startling against her skin and the whiteness of the sheets. He had trouble taking his eyes off of it.

The phone rang again and he got up, walking gingerly, self-conscious about his nakedness. He picked up the phone's handset and said, "hello."

There was silence for a second, then a click and dial tone. He dropped the handset back into its cradle.

Kitty was standing by the door, wrapped in a sheet. "Who was it?"

He shook his head. "I don't know. They hung up."

"It's the asshole, then," she said. "Goddammit. Just goddammit." She crossed her arms, gathering the sheet across her chest. "I'm getting pretty sick of this shit."

He said, "I'm sorry," which sounded weak, but was all he could think of.

She looked at the ceiling and puffed her cheeks out, making a sound like she was blowing off steam. Then she said, "It's OK, it's not your problem." She went back into the bedroom and he followed her and when she went into the bathroom he sat down on the bed and waited.

She came out a few minutes later with her hair combed and wearing a white terry robe. "How'd you like to go out?" she said.

He grabbed his watch from the table beside the bed. It was a little before one. "Not that much open. What'd you have in mind?"

"Anything. We could just ride." She put her hands into the robe's pockets and came and squatted down in front of him, using the pockets to keep the robe over her knees.

She looked up at him. "How 'bout it? Do a girl a favor?"

74

"Sure," he said, "Just let me put my pants back on."

"You got it." She leaned close to him without taking her hands out of the robe's pockets and, very gently, butted her forehead against his knee.

"You're a good man, Charlie Brown," she said.

★

He opened the truck door for her, and she smiled at him as she climbed in. He went around to the driver's side and when he reached to open the door someone stepped close to him from the far side of the dumpster. He stepped back, disconcerted, but the man stepped with him. Dave saw close-cut blond hair and a black T-shirt.

"Hey, Bud," the kid marine said. He jabbed Dave in the chest with his fingertips, just hard enough to hurt. "Who the hell do you think you are?" he said. Dave could smell beer on his breath. "Hey, hey," Dave said, holding his hands up, palms out. He tried to take another step back but the marine was right on top of him, pushing in close.

He poked again with his fingertips. "How about it, asshole? I asked you a question."

"Look," Dave said. He felt his heart racing and his tongue felt thick. It surprised him how suddenly afraid he was. Just an ex-marine. Just a kid with a black belt. "Look, I don't know what your problem is, but I think—"

"Bud, I don't give a shit what you think." Dave backed up against the truck and the marine followed. "I ought to cave your fucking head in."

Dave stopped backing and the marine loomed in his face. He didn't look as young close up. He looked drunk and cruel, his teeth clenched. "Look, friend," Dave said, and he saw the marine tense and drop back into a martial arts pose and he thought *This is it.* He found himself crouching, his fists balling up and the fear bringing acid up into his throat.

The marine kicked at him almost more quickly than he could follow, a booted foot flicking up at his stomach, and when he dropped his hands to protect himself it came again, a quick snap, the boot's sole stopping a few inches from his face. Dave crouched there, amazed that the kid seemed to have missed him altogether, though for an instant it seemed possible that he had been hit and somehow, incredibly, he just didn't feel it.

"Have you pissed yourself yet, asshole?" the marine said. "I'll bet you've shit in your pants, haven't you?"

The marine stepped close again, pointed a finger into Dave's face, two or three inches from his nose. Dave almost tried to hit him then, the muscles in his forearms jerking from holding back.

"You've lucked out, bud," the marine said. "I'm not going to break any of your bones, this time." Dave wanted to slap his hand away, spit in his face, but he couldn't quite make himself do it. He could feel his hands starting to shake and the muscles in his upper arms felt weak and tremulous. The marine backed away. "Stay the fuck away," the marine said. "I'm watching you, white trash."

That was more than Dave could take. "Fuck off, you little weasel," he said.

"Not nice," the marine said, and he stepped in quick and when Dave tried to cover his face punched Dave once, hard, in the stomach. Dave doubled over and fell to his knees, retching. The marine patted him on the back.

"Have a nice night," the marine said, and turned to walk away and Dave saw Kitty there, with the tire iron from under the truck's seat, and she swung it like a golf club from high above her shoulder. The marine said something that sounded like "oh," and then the socket end of the tire iron struck him in the temple and he collapsed sideways where he stood and hit the asphalt hard.

Dave blinked. He couldn't straighten up but he crabwalked, one hand on the ground, to the marine. Blood was running across the boy's forehead and into his eyes, and even in the reflected light from the streetlamps he could see that the eyes were half-open, dreamy and pale, the left one flooded with blood. "Aw, Christ," Dave said. He reached out to shake the boy's shoulder but found that he couldn't do it. His stomach throbbed and he thought he was going to throw up.

Kitty knelt down across from him. She put the tire iron down on the pavement. She touched the marine's face and turned it a little more into the light. Then she stood up again and Dave groaned and struggled up to his feet. She walked around the marine to Dave and touched his arm.

Dave said, "We ought to call an ambulance."

"You'll help me, OK?" she said. He nodded and felt her hand on his arm. She slid it down to his hand where he still held the keys to the truck clenched in his fist. She worked his hand open with her fingers and took them from him. Then she turned and ran back to the door of the apartment and went inside.

Dave crouched over the marine and waited. She was back quickly with a box and she put it into the bed of the truck. Then she took a towel out of the box and came over and picked up the tire iron and wrapped it in the towel. It looked, Dave thought, like the same pink towel that she had cried into when he'd first seen her. She opened the door of the truck and put the towel and tire iron on the seat. She stood just inside the door of the truck and Dave went to her.

"You don't have to go anywhere. It'll be all right."

"It's never all right," she said. Her voice was very sure and he didn't try to contradict her.

"Tell them you loaned me the truck, OK? Tell them you don't know where I went. Just go home, like you weren't even here."

"You don't have to go anywhere," he said again.

"OK," she said. She climbed into the truck and shut the door. Dave stepped back when the engine started, and he expected her to roll down the window and say something else to him but she didn't. She put the truck into gear and gave it gas and bumped out of the parking lot with a little screech of rubber. He watched his truck drive off through the shadows of the big, hanging oaks.

"I see *you*," he said out loud, though all he could see was the tree branch shadows where the truck's brake lights blinked once and were gone, and above that a few bright stars and the moon and its shadow blinking through the open spaces, coy as a doll's blind eye.

He walked off a few feet from where the marine lay and sat down on the pavement. The darkness settled around the streetlights. It was very still and he could hear the summer cicadas grinding away in the trees, one note higher than the sound of late-night traffic in the distance. The muscles in his stomach spasmed and he laid out flat on the asphalt. He needed to feel something solid underneath him but he was suddenly shaking so hard that the whole world seemed to shudder in sympathy. He wondered if somehow the ground itself really was trembling, ready to open up like a sinkhole and swallow him. He thought about the houses and the Porsches down somewhere in the darkness of the lime-stone cave whose collapsing roof had made that pretty little urban lake. It must be awfully quiet down there, so many years after the big excite-ment, just mud and catfish and expensive German cars, living rooms with throw rugs and TVs and pictures on the mantles. He closed his eyes and waited for the hollow earth to move him, his heart tight in his chest hoping it would.

MEMORIAL DAY

★ ★ ★

Samantha watches her sister, Naomi, rub the tabby, slowly, stroking her hand along the narrow back to the haunches, like milking a cow's teat. The morning before, Naomi had followed the cat through the wet grass behind the greenhouse, watched the cat's flanks bulge and strain until it dropped its litter, then took the wet sticky lumps and carefully broke each small neck, her fingers kneading the damp fur. "Nobody will want them," she had said. "It's only merciful."

Samantha watches Naomi stroke the tabby, and she waits for her brother to come and take from her the responsibility of their sister. David is coming to take Samantha and Naomi to Washington, D.C. to see the Vietnam Memorial and Naomi's husband's name inscribed on the great wall of black granite.

"She's still so weak," Naomi says.

"Why in God's name haven't you gotten that cat fixed?" Samantha says, but without much heat.

The cat purrs and rubs at Naomi's hands, snuffles at her knotted fingers. "Because it's cruel," Naomi says.

Samantha says nothing. She cannot deal with paradox, and she can no longer deal with her own sister. Samantha has been with her sister, in her sister's house, for seven days, and she is tired. Naomi is recovering from a hysterectomy, and though she isn't demanding and doesn't complain, Samantha is still anxious for David to come, so she won't have to cope with Naomi alone. It frightens Samantha that a few deformed cells on a glass slide have cost her sister her uterus. Naomi seems still so young. It bothers Samantha, as well, that Naomi seems so unconcerned, as if the operation were only something she allowed because the doctor had insisted, as if the loss of her womb were nothing to her. Samantha believes that Naomi has become less than sane, that she has lived alone with pain too long for her mind to be entirely sound. Samantha has come to Tallahassee from Miami because her sister is unable to take care of herself and she is afraid that soon Naomi will again need or want no one but herself.

"Dave will be here soon," Samantha says. "It'll be good for all of us, getting together again. And God knows, we can all afford to get away and see a little of the country."

Naomi picks up the cat, lifting it from underneath its front legs, and holds it before her, as if she is talking to the cat. "I know. I just don't like traveling much. You know, planes, bad food. Too much of everything."

"Well, yes," Samantha says evenly, "but that's not the point. And Dave has already bought the plane tickets." Naomi's husband, Michael, was killed in the war back in the fall of 1972, and Samantha is hopeful that seeing the new memorial in Washington will draw her sister out, maybe bring on some sort of catharsis. She suspects her sister is still haunted by Michael. She thinks the trip to Washington, seeing the memorial, his name, will exorcise him.

Naomi sets the cat on the floor and its sits there for a time, grooming, then it jumps up on the back of the ratty couch and stretches out in a square of sunlight from a dusty bay window. When the silence begins to sit in the room like some great, dark animal, Samantha leaves her sister watching the cat sun and goes to the front porch to watch for David. The trip could only be therapeutic, she thinks. She is suddenly glad for the cancer that has made Naomi need her, that has forced her only sister to acknowledge her. She watches the sun settle and touch the tops of the pecan trees that stand beside the drive. The evening is warm, and she can see the dust rising slowly through the heat at the end of the drive, though she cannot yet see the car. The dust is solid, a moving thing. The roses in the yard are neat and weeded, and make her think of a cemetery.

★

Washington is loud and crowded, the day cool and thin. David rents a car and finds the luggage while Naomi and Samantha sit together in the terminal. Samantha holds Naomi's hand, and Naomi lets her, but her hand is cool and loose in Samantha's. David drives them to the hotel and Samantha keeps her window down despite the cold to escape his cigarette smoke.

Samantha helps Naomi up to their room while David carries his bag to his room on another floor. Naomi is flushed, and when they get to the room she goes to bathroom and is quietly sick. It is only then that Samantha realizes that the traveling has been hard on Naomi. When she is through, Samantha sits on the bed beside her and wipes her face with a damp washcloth.

"I'll be all right," Naomi tells her after a time.

"I know," Samantha says. "Just sit for a while."

Naomi nods and lets Samantha press the cloth to her forehead. Naomi's eyes close and Samantha blows gently against her temple where the blood flushes close to the skin's surface.

In the morning, David drives them all to the Mall, where the new memorial has been built. The green is crowded with veterans in fatigues and tennis shoes, in wheelchairs, some of them, and on crutches. Samantha and David lead Naomi down to the huge, black, granite V that is the monument and they walk slowly through the crowd that mills in front of it. For the first time Naomi looks frightened and overwhelmed, and Samantha holds her hand while David looks for one of the men who have the indexes to the names on the monument.

"I'm not up to this," Naomi tells Samantha. She looks very frail suddenly, covering her eyes with one pale hand.

"David will be back in just a minute," Samantha says gently. She did

81

not sleep well and she feels exhausted, a deep, tired pain that has taken root in her spine. Samantha sees David among the crowd next to the monument. He waves to her and she takes Naomi's hand and leads her down to where he is standing, his hand against the black stone wall.

"I've found him," David says. He smiles and taps his hand against a line of names near the center. "I've found him."

"It's just a name," Naomi says. She walks stiffly, as if she is very old. She walks, Samantha thinks, like there is something inside of her that will not let her go, something that Naomi holds close like a relic, something Samantha cannot see or understand. Samantha thinks about Michael, about his one and only name among the thousands of stark names etched on the shiny black stone. She cannot remember what her sister's husband looked like, who he was. It seems incredible to her that Naomi could still be so possessed by the idea of someone Samantha can't even recall. It is as if Naomi had lived her entire life in the small time she had had with this man who is to Samantha no more than a vague memory, as if Naomi had lived all of her pain all at once and is now only waiting for the empty, painless years to pass. It comes to Samantha then, some inkling of what she realizes is the truth, an intuition of just how fortunate Naomi is, just how stunningly beautiful the accommodation is that Naomi has made with the world. A thing of wonder that leaves her breathless.

Naomi lingers against the black of the wall, only a little way from Samantha. David has moved on somewhere out of her line of sight, following the rigid rows of names. She knows that her brother and her sister will bear her good intentions until she loves them away, back into their own lives. It's only merciful, Naomi had said. The day is bright and hot and Samantha shades her eyes with a hand and waits for them to come back to her.

TRASH FISH

★ ★ ★

onny sat in the front of the boat with the rods and waited for his father to figure the motor out. The woman had never left the doorway; she'd taken Raye's money and pointed a finger down the path to the river. "Boat's in the water," was all she'd said, and then she'd eased the door nearly shut, keeping an eye on them through the crack as if she thought they'd try something on her if she weren't careful.

"What are we trying to catch?" Donny asked. He wanted to know what kind of fish—catfish, bass, crappie, bluegill? Raye had bought a Styrofoam cup full of nightcrawlers from the boat woman, but that didn't mean much. You could catch anything on worms.

"Fish" is all Raye would say.

"Hell," Donny mumbled, but he waited until Raye was pulling the cord to crank the engine before he mumbled it.

The engine sputtered and died. Raye fiddled with the choke and pulled again and it caught with a gurgling roar.

"Push off," Raye ordered, so Donny did, stepping over the rods back onto the bank, where he shoved at the boat's flat bow until the mud let it go. He tried to get back in but his foot slipped on the seat and he fell to his knees in the shallow water.

"Stop screwing around and get in the goddamn boat," Raye growled.

"OK, OK." His father, he could tell, was in a rare mood. He climbed in over the rods and held on while Raye opened the throttle and headed the boat upriver.

The night settled in between the trees on either bank. Donny watched for water moccasins in the overhanging branches but found pretty quickly he couldn't tell a snake from a limb in the dimness. He'd heard stories about moccasins dropping into the laps of unwary fishermen and the idea of it made him feel more than a little uneasy.

Raye killed the engine and let the boat ride upstream a ways on its own momentum. For a long moment the silence was nearly absolute, just the lapping of the water, and then the little peeper frogs started in and an anhinga called mournfully off somewhere in the darkness upriver. Donny looked around and couldn't see anything about this particular piece of the river that set it apart from any other, but he figured Raye knew what he was doing.

"Toss that anchor out on the bank," Raye told him. The "anchor" was a galvanized steel bucket filled with concrete. One end of a length of rope was tied onto the bucket's handle, the other end through an eyebolt screwed into the boat's bow. Donny picked up the bucket and heaved it at the muddy bank as they drifted past. It landed at the water's edge with a wet thump.

"Higher up," Raye said. "It ain't never going to hold, you leave it there."

"Hell, Dad—" Donny started.

"Just do it," Raye said, and the tone of his voice said, *just do it before I kick your ass clean out of this boat.*

The current had pulled the boat back downstream and pulled the anchor rope tight. Donny hauled the anchor into the water and pulled it hand over hand toward the boat; it came easily enough for a minute, bumping along the river bottom, but then it hung on something underwater and as hard as Donny strained against the rope, it wouldn't budge.

"Anchor's stuck."

Raye looked up from pumping up the lantern. "Well, you're going to have to go get it, then, aren't you."

"Dad—"

"You hung it up, you go get it. I've already given that nigger woman ten bucks for this piece of shit boat, I'm not paying for that thing, too," Raye said, gesturing out to where the rope angled down into the water. "'Sides, you're already wet. You ain't gonna get no wetter."

Donny knew better than to argue. He thought about taking off his tennis shoes, and then thought maybe he wouldn't. There was no telling what was on the river bottom, and like Raye said, they weren't going to get any wetter than they already were. He looked over the side of the boat but couldn't really see much. The moon had started to rise and bits and streaks of moonlight that had made it through the trees gleamed dully on the water. He put a leg over the side and eased himself into the water, the boat tilting toward him enough that Raye cussed and put the lantern down and waited for him to get all the way in.

The water was cold, but not unpleasantly so, and deep enough that he couldn't touch bottom, though they were only ten or twelve yards from the bank. He hung from the side of the boat and felt for the anchor rope with his free hand. He pulled on the rope a couple of times, but he knew it wasn't going to move and he knew he was going to have to dive down in the dark water and find the stupid anchor and work it out from under whatever stump or snag it was under. He thought once about water moccasins and whatever else might be swimming around with him, and then put them out of his mind and dove down, kicking hard, letting the rope slide through his hand.

It was harder to follow the rope down to the bottom that he thought he would be. He couldn't see anything at all in the water and the nylon rope was slick. He came back to the surface, took another breath, and then hauled himself down quick, hand over hand, so as to keep his own buoyancy from lifting him away from the rope. He kept his eyes closed in the water since he couldn't see anything, anyway. The bottom came up more quickly than he thought it would, though, and he jammed his fingers painfully into the concrete in the bucket and let go of the rope and then couldn't find it again. For a long, panicky second he didn't know which way was up, everything all around him equally black.

Then light suddenly bloomed around him, bright as some sort of revelation, cutting through the water in brilliant streaks. His mind didn't want to take it in. It was like angels coming for him deep down in the river. For a couple of heartbeats, he couldn't move at all; he just hung, breathless, the lights shifting all around him in the water, weirdly prismatic. Then realization hit: it was the lantern. Raye had gotten it lit and was holding it up over the side of the boat. Donny looked straight up into it, dazzling as a star, and kicked hard and rose and broke through the surface with a gasp.

He held onto the boat's gunwale and looked up under his brows at his father's face hovering behind the blinding glare of the lantern.

"You get it?"

Donny blew his breath out through his teeth. "No," he said. He sighed bitterly and felt for the rope again. "No," he muttered under his breath, so Raye couldn't hear him, "I did not get it, I did not get shit except almost fucking drowned in a goddamned river for a goddamned two dollar bucket filled with concrete."

He sucked in a deep breath and dove, going down the rope hand over hand again. The bottom came up full of sharp shadows, the vague light of the lantern making the darkness at its edges seem even thicker. The bucket was wedged under a branch half-buried in the river bottom. He worked it loose and dropped it again, then kicked hard and swam back up to the surface.

Raye helped him back into the boat by grabbing the back of his belt and hauling him up. "You look like a wet rat, boy."

"Thanks," Donny said, careful to keep the sarcasm out of his voice. He pulled the anchor up out of the water and swung it by the rope back and forth to get up momentum, then threw it out well back into the weeds on the bank.

"All right, then," Raye said approvingly.

Donny wiped as much water off of himself with his hands as he could, then put his shirt back on. "Hell," he said.

"Here," Raye said. He handed Donny an open Coke and Donny could smell the rum in it. "You better rig your pole."

Donny drank off some of his drink, gasping at how strong Raye had mixed it. Goddamn old man, he thought. There was nothing to him but drink and nastiness. Shameless old son of a bitch. Not a pretentious bone in him, though. Raye McLaughlin was who he was, and he never seemed the least inclined to apologize for it. Everybody in Mascotte Grove knew Raye, and Donny knew that most of them respected him. He was a tough old shit, and people talked about how slick he used to be, a wheeler-dealer, somebody who got what he wanted and did what he said he was going to do. Raye had said once while Donny was listening, "They might talk shit about me, but they never talk shit to me."

That was it; everyone was made tentative by Raye, his own son included. It wasn't so much his physical strength as his attitude, Donny thought, the certain knowledge you found in yourself when you were with him that, so far as Raye was concerned, you could drop off the face of the earth and he not only wouldn't much care, he wouldn't much notice.

When Donny was eight he had found three spaniel-mix puppies someone had dumped on the side of the highway. There had been five, but two had already been hit by cars. He had taken the dogs to his mother, who'd said they ought to be drowned because they were mutts and they were ratty and they were about half dead. But she'd helped him clean them up and she'd fed them and put them in a box with a scrap of quilt. One of the pups died overnight, and they'd let one of the other two be adopted. Then Donny had pestered his mother mercilessly for three days running until she'd agreed to let him keep the last one. He'd named the dog Happy, more from wishful thinking than because the dog was especially cheerful; in fact the puppy had never seemed to get over the trauma of being abandoned and half starved and nearly run down by cars, and he had grown into a nervous and snappish dog.

Raye hadn't even seemed to notice Happy was around except at supper time, when he'd make Donny put the dog out because he couldn't stand it watching him eat. Other than at meals, Happy spent most of his time curled up under the TV stand; the sound of the programs seemed to comfort him, and Raye didn't seem to mind the dog watching him watch television. Then Happy had made the mistake of growling at Raye one evening when Raye stepped in a little too close to change the channels and Raye cussed and kicked him hard and when Happy tried to scurry out from under the TV stand, Raye shoved the TV off its stand on top of Happy, breaking the TV and Happy's hip in one furious stroke. Happy had lived the rest of his life with a limp, and had lived it outside, where he spent most of his time in the crawl space under the trailer, beneath the TV room, a little removed from but still near the somewhat muffled comfort of the television's constant susurrus.

Happy had died when Donny was nine or ten. He'd found a canebrake rattler in the backyard under a persimmon tree and had barked long enough at it to get Donny out, and Donny went to get Raye. Raye had killed the snake with a hoe; it had tried to slip away after Donny had dragged Happy back and Raye had caught it before it could coil again and chopped its head off with one clean stroke of the blade. Then Raye had taken the snake's body inside to gut and skin it in the kitchen sink.

Donny had gone back to the dark spot of persimmon-tree shade where the head still lay to take a look. Happy had come up to sniff the snake's severed head (Donny had let him go after he'd seen that the rattler was dead) and before Donny could even blink, the snake's gulletless mouth had snapped open like a hinge and buried its fangs in poor Happy's soft, black nose. Happy had dashed, yelping, back underneath the trailer where, underneath the constant muttering of the television, he convulsed and died.

It took Donny a while to make up his mind to go under the house after the dog. He was scared of the darkness under there and the black widow spiders and possibility of other snakes; he was also afraid of Happy's death, which he knew would linger in that narrow space the way that his grandmother's larger death had lingered, first throughout the house, then constricting itself down over the weeks and months until it was just a quiet breath of stillness in her own small room. Death, he knew, was a tangible thing. Death, he knew, abides.

But he'd gone under there and brought Happy out, poor stupid dog curled up in a tight fetal coil, hard as a truck tire. All Raye had had to say about it was, "Well goddamn, look at that." Then he'd gone back inside the house. Donny had buried Happy out in a pasture, the rattlesnake's head forever clamped on his nose. Raye had had Donny's mother fry up the snake for supper that night, though Donny and his mother both had had cornbread and buttermilk instead and left the eating of the rattler to Raye.

Donny looked at his father threading a nightcrawler onto a treble hook. *Jesus*, he thought, and shivered in his damp clothes. Goddamned old man. Not all that old, really, he guessed; he realized he really didn't know his own father's age, didn't even, come to think of it, know Raye's birthday. June, he thought. Nineteen-forty something. Probably. There hadn't ever been much in the way of birthday parties in his family. It seemed odd to think of Raye as even having a birthday. Birthdays were happy times for regular, sentimental, frivolous people, and Raye was none of those things. Hard old bastard, Donny thought. And him out here fishing like it was something that mattered, like he'd even wanted to fish in the first place, that anything mattered to him anymore but the booze. Sad. Raye stood up with a groan and heaved his bait out over the water, the line singing as it paid out of the reel, the bait hitting the water with a flat plop.

A strange feeling came over Donny; a melancholy all mixed up with something akin to affection seemed to seep into him from somewhere, passing through him like a chill.

He yanked the tackle box around so he wouldn't have to think about it. He dug through the rusty lures and pulled out a big bucktail jig. He tied it on and swung the lure out over the side of the boat. Raye had the set the bail on his reel and was watching Donny get ready to cast.

"That's a striper lure," he said, "you won't catch shit with that."

"I don't know. Maybe."

"*I* know. Put a treble hook on and a sinker."

"I thought I'd try it."

"There's no goddamn stripers out there. Suit yourself, you want to waste your time."

Donny knew he was probably right. He'd picked the jig on impulse, not knowing really what it was supposed to catch. But he felt an obligation to be stubborn about it now. He stood up and swung the rod back and made a mighty cast. The heavy jig sailed up and across the river and plopped into the water at the very edge of the lantern's light. He cranked hard to get the lure away from the shallows near the bank before it could snag something, then worked it slowly through the water back up to the boat.

Raye shook his head and said, "shit," when Donny pulled the lure up out of the water and cast it out again.

The jig hit the water and sank and just as Donny turned the crank to close the bail on the reel something grabbed it and ran. The line howled out of the reel so furiously Donny couldn't even think about what to do next. He held the crank in place with one hand and fumbled at the drag with the other, trying to tighten it down and stop the line from stripping out of the reel so frighteningly fast.

"Leave the drag alone! Set the goddamned hook!" Raye yelled. Donny hauled back on the rod to set the hook and Raye yelled again: "Not so damned hard! All you're gonna get is lips you yank that hard!"

The fish slowed its run and Donny pumped the crank arm, taking in line until he thought he might be making it get close enough to the boat to net it, and then the fish took off again, making the line sing as it stripped back out again. It slowed again and he cranked the line back in. Then it ran again and he started the process all over. His forearms started to ache and he could feel his father hovering near him watching what he was doing, though he didn't dare look away from the rod where it bent over toward the water in a fierce and straining arch. The fish broke through the surface ten or fifteen yards upriver and he could see the lantern light glint silver off its scales as the fish rolled, long and sleek as an eel, trying to throw the hook. He heard Raye let out his breath in a disgusted snort.

"What is it?" Donny asked over his shoulder, working the fish.

"Just a fucking gar. Trash fish."

"It's huge," Donny said. He guessed it must be three feet long, maybe forty or fifty pounds.

"Don't matter. You can't eat it, it ain't worth catching."

"You don't want it?"

"Nobody wants it. That's the white trash of fish you got. That's bony, bloody shit nobody's gonna eat. Nobody except a nigger would eat a gar."

Raye sat back down and Donny could feel his father's disgust, a palpable thing settling into the boat with them.

"Should I cut the line?"

"Hell, no. Get the lure back."

Donny cranked the reel and the fish, played out, let itself be brought up to the side of the boat. He pulled the rod up and raised the gar's wolfish head up out of the water, silver scales the size of dimes and jagged rows of teeth arranged around the lure where it hooked into its long jaw.

"How am I supposed to get that?"

"You just get it," Raye said. He pulled an old, cracked oar up from where it ran under the seats and moved carefully to Donny's end of the boat with it. Donny dragged the fish against the boat's side and Raye swung the oar and smacked the fish hard with it. The fish flopped a couple of times and then hung loose on the line.

Raye leaned over the fish, tipping the gunwale down dangerously close to the water in the process, and pushed his fingers into the fish's gills and lifted it up enough to get slack in the line so he could unhook the lure. Just as he reached for the lure, the fish came alive again and with a flopping twist it took off the tip of Raye's index finger. Raye fell back with a shriek and very nearly knocked Donny clean out of the boat.

"Jesus H. Christ on a crutch!" Raye bellowed, struggling to get himself up from the mucky water in the boat's bottom. "God damn!" He cradled his injured hand against his chest and the fish thumped, battering its bloody head against the side of the boat as if it were drumming out some sort of piscine warning to the rest of its tribe.

Then Raye picked up the oar again. Donny could see a spot of blood the size of an orange on the front of his shirt. He swung the oar down on the gar with a grunt and a roar, hitting it so hard against the boat's side that its belly split redly open. Then he put the oar down again and pressed his hand against his chest. "Shit," he said, and then, "get the damned lure and let's go home."

Donny pushed his hand gingerly into the fish's gills, and waited for it to come alive one more time, like Happy's rattlesnake head, but it stayed dead. He put the rod down and worked the lure gingerly out of the gar's jaw and let the fish's corpse drop back into the water. He watched the long carcass roll away downstream in the current, slowly sinking, until it escaped the circle of lantern light and disappeared. He kept looking even after it was gone, still feeling it in the muscles of his forearms where he'd fought it, the live weight down below, struggling against him somewhere deep in the dark heart of the river.

Raye had Donny fix him a drink and he gulped it down and then started the engine one-handed and nosed the boat into the bank so Donny could yank the anchor up out of the weeds. Then they headed back down the river to the little landing with its shack and its burned out trailer house shadowy against the one weak light that marked it in the dark. The door to the shack stayed closed and they left the boat as it was where Raye had run it up onto the flat, muddy bank. Raye finished off another rum and Coke while Donny loaded the tackle back into the car's trunk.

Donny watched while Raye sat on the edge of the car seat and poured raw rum over the bloody end of his finger. He yelped and swore and shook his hand wildly, and then he showed it to Donny in the dim illumination from the car's dome light. "Boy," he said, his voice a little tired, Donny thought, a little defeated, "this is just the price you pay for your pleasures." Then he wrapped it up in his handkerchief and handed Donny the bottle of rum.

"Make me a drink, will you," he told Donny, "and you can drive us back, if you think you can do it without running us into a ditch."

I can indeed, Donny thought, and he did, Raye drunk and snoring most of the way, the big Ford sailing through the darkness like a barge on the black river of the county road, following the trees and telephone poles as they scattered in and out of the headlights ahead. The Ford's big V-8 surged when he gave it gas, blowing wide around the curves with nothing ahead but the night and the faraway moon high in the sky like a milk jug anchored on the pinholed surface of the night.

And as he passed through town, the streetlights flashed in through the windows, regular as a metronome, and he looked over and saw Raye grinning at him, his hurt hand cradled against his chest.

"You're doing all right, aren't you boy?" Raye said, still grinning, his eyes yellow and sad in the brief, dim sputters of light.

"Sure," Donny told him.

Later, thinking about it, Donny would feel a sudden rush of grief, thinking of his father there, watching him drive, filled with liquor and despair and with the harsh and atavistic instinct of what Donny would long after come to realize was his love. This is what we have, he would think: something as intangible as flickers of light lingering in the depths of deep water, bright and lonely as angels. That's all there ever is, all that matters when we come to it, our blood silted up like a river with its shadows.

At the time, though, he just said *Jesus* under his breath and concentrated on his driving, the town and its lights dropping away on either side and the road ahead stretching out before them, carrying them away together into the darkness and the long night.

SWIMMING THE CAVE

★ ★ ★

She's here because she wants to be. She's sure of that. She's here, she thinks, because she needs to know how far he'll go for her. She's here because she's pretty sure already how far she'll go for him. Pretty far, she thinks. Far.

The water is greenish but clear, so clear she can see the bottom down below and limbs that have fallen off the orange trees that stand all around the sinkhole. The sand is warm under her bare feet; there's a little breeze blowing through the grove, and that makes her shiver, though the breeze is warm, too. He's sitting on the limestone lip of the sinkhole, and she can see how the edge presses into the skin of his bare rear where he sits, seventeen, naked, dangling his feet into the water, looking at her.

She's hiding, feeling shy. An orange tree leans in over the pool, roots torn out in an arc, and she's standing in the little pit it has left in the sand where it was uprooted, the bare roots like a screen between herself and him, so he can only see her face, or maybe a little more through the snaky tangle. She crosses her arms over her breasts to hide the embarrassing darkness of her nipples. She watches him. He grins at her, and says something, just loud enough that she can almost hear it, so that she has to study the way he mouths the words to understand him, and his mouth, moving around the words, makes a thrill tickle in her stomach in a way that's almost uncomfortable. *C'mon*, he says, *feels good.*

OK, she tells him.

She edges around the screen of roots and feels how her bareness grows. She steps up onto the tree trunk and walks heel-to-toe up its incline to where the branches begin, all of them still hung with green fruit hard as tumors. She sits down quickly, sidesaddle on the rough trunk, arms crossed over her breasts, knees gathered up to chest, heels together and tucked hard against herself so nothing shows that matters. Oh boy, she tells herself. Oh, Jesus. But for him she knows that she's the one, her blond hair slick as cornsilk, green eyes, skin the shy blue of milk. She knows. She can see the way his eyes narrow. The way he breathes through his mouth, his lips just a little apart.

Watch, he says, and this is what she's come for. He's going to show her. No big deal, he's done it before, but it scares her enough she can't wait to see him do it, just for her. He grins. He slips into the water. He takes three quick, deep breaths. Then he ducks his head under the water and dives so suddenly she can feel him inside her heart, the way the cold takes hold of him, the water around his head tight as a fist. He pounds down toward the bottom and she can feel in her stomach how he pushes down against the fearful, buoyant part of himself, swimming down to the cave, dark spot, quiet, limestone ribbed and arcing like a trachea to another sinkhole fifteen yards away.

He goes. He's gone. She closes her eyes and feels it slip moss-greased around him like a foreskin, old hat, old friend, been here before, *no big deal. Push through*, she thinks, wiggle the hips, toes jammed against the slippery floor. Easy. His life magnifies itself under the water's thin skin, undulant with sun.

She jumps down from the trunk, runs through the trees over the sand to the other sinkhole to wait for him, shivering as she slides into the cold water, her hands fluttering like leaves to keep her afloat, a cold space in her chest where she dreams love is, waiting to be filled.

And then she feels him go breathless inside herself, something like a lump of stone against her womb pressing a single, cetacean grunt of surprise out of the darkness. She can feel the world all at once begin to dwindle to a gray button of light hung like the maiden moon above her, here where she waits just for him, for all of his young and unconsidered life bitten through like a tongue, flat in his mouth where his breath used to be.

No, she tells herself, don't be silly. But there's a pain inside her head like depth whining in the bones behind her jaw, in the small bones of her ear. Something holds him, elbow and shoulder, tight inside itself.

The water is so cold she can't breathe. She wills his shoulders to unjoint themselves, his tumid heart to swallow in one, hard-wrung gulp. She knows, absolutely, that all it would take to make him come back to her is just a word, an appeal not even to God but to possibility hovering over every young life like a gift. If she could just say it. If she knew what it was and could say it out loud like a confession for all the world to hear.

For one instant she thinks he's free. Her eyes open. She's sure she sees him, rising, amazed, lifted on the foam of his upward breath, soaring underneath her where her legs sway and part like wings, like everything he has ever wanted, desire sharp as the thin needles of water driving themselves through his ears into the place behind his eyes where the stars crawl in their darkness.

He's coming, she thinks. And she will be there for him, love generous and full, sweet as mercy, waiting to go ass-bare with him into the rumpled grass. There's nothing to prove, she'll tell him, nothing I need to know I don't already know.

He'll be breathing hard. She'll be crying for him. *Lie still* she will tell him. *Deep breath. There.*

Her hair slick as cornsilk, bare skin soft as moss, smelling of water. The air all around her is lush with her waiting, humid like exhaled breath. He's coming, she knows it. She's never doubted it. He will come and she will hold him fiercely to her always, elbow and shoulder, skin bare and cool, eyes forever green under a sinking crescent of trees.

HAPPY PUPPY

★　　★　　★

L ife had been good. He and Lucy had lived in apartments for a while, and when she had finished her degree and the future had started to look certain, they bought the house, brand-new and white-stuccoed, sitting plump against a lake full of motorboats and skiers and aging bass fishermen. Jack had been happy, for a while. He had gone to work, put in his day in front of a glowing CRT. He had fertilized his lawn and grown azaleas. Not bad for a boy out of Mascotte Grove, the capital of backwater, trailer-trash nowhere.

Tonight, he microwaves a dinner and he and the dog go out on the back lawn and share it. Then he just sits for a while in the lawn chair and watches the lights shatter on the chop in the water. Mosquitoes drone tirelessly in his ears.

There are still a few lights on the lake, bass fisherman working the water hyacinth, hoping for a late-evening lunker. The dog whines at the june bugs that are beginning to swarm around the porch light, clicking their hard shells against the glass. He sits up suddenly and cocks his head, as if he has heard one of those sounds only dogs can hear. Then he trots out into the darkness of the neighbor's backyard.

Jack falls asleep in the lawn chair, his chin on his chest like a drunk.

He wakes up that way, too, with a start, and for a panicky instant he thinks he's behind the wheel of the car, that he's fallen asleep driving. In the darkness, the concerted murmur of heat-pump fans sounds like tire rubber humming on pavement.

He calls for the dog and listens for the telltale spurs-jangling sound of the tags on Hoover's collar. Then he walks halfway around the lake through people's backyards, creeping uneasily in the moonless dark around jungle gyms and barbecue grills, whistling every once in a while in that five-note demand he'd learned from his father calling bird dogs and to which Jack had taught the dog to answer. The bushes are still loaded with water from the afternoon's rain and every time he touches something, fat leaf-smelling drops shower down on him in a miniature storm.

He jogs back to the house and gets his keys and sets out through the neighborhood looking for the dog, driving slowly with the window rolled down. Every once in while headlights loom up in his rearview mirror and hang there for a while, close, until the driver figures out he isn't going to be able to intimidate Jack into speeding up, then he or she tears off around him. One fellow yells something that gets lost in the tire squeal and engine roar.

Then one car pulls in close but doesn't go around. After he has followed Jack for a block or so, Jack taps on the brake pedal a couple of times to tell him to Get Off My Ass and go around. Flashing blue lights bloom suddenly above the headlights.

"Aw, shit," he says, feeling the frightened little jumps of paranoia start in his bowels. It's something instinctive, he thinks, that makes us fear cops even when we've done nothing wrong. Or the fact that deep down we all know we're guilty of something dark enough to be criminal, even if we don't remember it.

He pulls over to the curb. After he's stopped he opens his door and starts to get out. He read somewhere that cops are less likely to hassle you that way, if you stand eye-to-eye with them instead of sitting in your car while they stand over you. It's supposed to be like with dogs, he guesses, dominance and submission.

As he puts one foot out, a voice crackles through a PA, telling him to *please remain in the vehicle*. He sits back in the car, then closes the door and waits for the cop to do whatever it is cops do when they pull you over before they confront you, call in the license plate, probably. Blue lights flicker and roll across the dashboard, filling the car with skittery little shadows.

After a while a brighter light brushes across the back of his neck and into the seat beside him. The cop walks up with a big, black flashlight in one hand, held up above her shoulder, the way someone might hold a spear or a vaulting pole, playing its beam around the inside of the car. She shines it in his eyes for a moment, then lets the beam drop. He sees she's wearing black driving gloves, the kind that leave the back of the hand bare. A big, chrome-plated revolver sits comfortably in a holster high on her hip.

"License and registration, please," she says briskly.

Jack has to lean across to get the registration out of the glove box. The flashlight beam comes back up and focuses on his hand as he digs around for the registration papers. Someone moves outside the passenger window of the car and he is a little surprised to see a second cop, a man, standing there, back just a bit, watching him. He looks tense. One hand rests casually—very casually, the thumb hooked over his belt—on top of his gun.

No damned wonder people are paranoid around cops. He fishes the papers out and sits up straight again, handing them over to the first cop along with his license.

She points the flashlight at them and looks them over in its glare. "May I ask where you're going, sir?" she says without looking up.

"I lost my dog," he says. It sounds lame even to him. "He ran off, so I'm driving around looking. I think he might be around here."

"Do you live in this area, sir?"

Jack gestures over his shoulder. "Back a few blocks. On the lake. Did I do something?"

"That's what we're trying to find out, sir," she says.

He feels chilled by that. "Is there a problem?" he asks.

Instead of answering she cocks her head to one side to talk into the radio microphone clipped to the front of her left shoulder. It squawks back at her and she hands him back his license and registration.

"There've been a few burglaries in the area, sir," she says, and snaps the flashlight off. "You were driving a little suspiciously. I don't think there's a problem, but you probably ought to go on home. If your dog's loose, the chances are good he's been picked up already. We find half-a-dozen a night out here. I'd check with the City Animal Shelter in the morning and see if they've got him."

"I will. Is that all? You thought I was casing houses?"

"Something like that," she says. "Good night, sir."

He watches her in his side mirror as she walks back to the cruiser. She and the male officer say something to each other across the car's roof, then both climb in. The blue lights go out.

He starts the car and waits for them to come around. After a minute or so of that, he realizes they are waiting for him. He puts the car into gear and pulls carefully out into the street. They follow him the rest of the way home, then drive off as he pulls into the garage.

Once he's inside the house he finds himself wanting to peek through the blinds to see if they have come back around and are parked out front, but he resists the impulse. It would be disappointing if they weren't there, and he is pretty sure they won't be. Once he'd proved his connection to the neighborhood, he rose, he is sure, through the simple act of placing himself among the homeowning middle class, above suspicion of any serious sort.

Except, of course, he is going to lose his house. The real estate agent, an old friend from high school, is coming by in the morning. Remembering that makes him feel suddenly just a bit dispossessed, a little more vulnerable. Without the house, even just looking for his dog after dark makes him seem guilty.

It is a bracing thought, unpleasant but necessary. He feels clear-eyed now, and aware. He knows where he stands.

★

He wakes up to the sound of hammering and thinks one of the neighbors must be up to something, but it's Darien he sees when he peers through the blinds, hammering a For Sale sign into the dead grass of his front lawn.

He watches her work, tapping at the top of the sign's frame with a claw hammer, first on one side and then the other, keeping both legs of the frame even.

Even in her real estate uniform, he realizes, she looks good. The mid-thirties-softening that makes most of the neighborhood wives seem a little overfed has been good to her. She looks a little less like the high school cross-country runner he remembers, lean and starved, and a little more tempting.

He pulls his jeans on and goes out to see her. She looks up when the door opens and waves the hammer at him.

"Hi," she says, then she points at the yard, shaking the hammer at it. "You know, you could take better care of this place."

"Hi, yourself. I know I could. Six months ago I had the best lawn out here, Bermuda-grass heaven, edged like a razor. Somehow I've just lost interest in grass since then."

She leans the hammer against the sign and dusts her hands. "I guess I can understand that. You going to invite me in?"

"You going to make comments about the inside, too?"

"Heaven forbid."

"Yeah, sure. Come on in. Watch for dogshit coming across, though."

"I always do."

She walks across to the door. He notes she is smart enough to wear flats when she works. A lot of time on her feet walking across soft lawns. Sensible. He decides he likes sensible, despite the fact that he'd thought of Lucy that way, too. Sensible had made him despair of Lucy, finally. Had made her despair of him, too. Once he'd lost his job, once Bryson Technical Engineering had decided one fine March afternoon that they needed one less mediocre tech-writer to write copy for their instruction manuals, he'd become someone she couldn't understand anymore. He was unproductive, home too much, a little depressed. He could hardly move himself to do anything for a while, and Lucy had had little use for that, and after a time—a long time, he had to admit—she'd discovered she had little use for him. She'd looked at him one day on her way out the door to work and he understood without her having to say a word. *This is it?* she was asking herself, *this is all there is?*

Darien wrinkled her nose at the mess of dishes and old newspapers strewn around the living room. "What do you do here all day? Other than shaving and lawn work, I mean."

"Sit around with my hands in my pockets, mostly," he says, "about what you'd expect."

"Have you gotten hold of Lucy?"

"Sort of. I've called her mother's place. Her mother won't let me talk to her. I've told Helen—Lucy's mother—I need to sell the house, and she said Lucy would go along with that, after her lawyer reads the papers. She hadn't been giving me anything for this place anyway. Which is why I haven't made a payment in six months. So I guess it's OK. She won't even let me talk to Jay. Helen won't."

"Do you see him?"

"Once every two weeks, like clockwork. She drops him off without really slowing down, and then we spend a lousy day together trying to be Superdad and His Still-Faithful Offspring. Then she zips by and blows the horn and he's gone for another two weeks."

"You're not getting divorced?"

"Not yet. I don't know why. There's not even anything official about the separation. Lucy doesn't want to talk to me, but she hasn't called a lawyer, at least so far as I know."

"You'd know. You don't mind me asking this stuff do you? I mean, it's none of my business, but it might affect how we handle the house. And of course, I'm nosy. And worried about you."

"Hell no, I don't mind. Don't worry about me, though. I come from finest kind of white trash. Resilient. We wear well. Like Naugahyde. Tough and unnatural."

She gives him a look. "You're sure a smartass when you're unhappy."

"Who's unhappy?"

"Christ." She shuffles the papers back together and holds them out to him. "Get these to Lucy. Get her to sign the listing agreement in front of a notary. Then get back to me and we'll get this place on the market. I wouldn't screw around too long. The banks don't have much patience these days with folks who let their mortgage payments lapse. To them, you're just another deadbeat."

"Ouch."

She sighs and lets one shoulder droop. It makes her look discouraged and he suddenly feels very tired. He lets his eyes close. When he opens them she's looking at him.

"You really ought to talk to somebody."

"Yeah, I know." He walks over to the sink. "You want some coffee?"

"No. I ought to get going." He has his back to her while he fiddles around in the sink, looking for a relatively clean cup, but he can feel her waiting for him to say something.

"I was really surprised when you called me," she says then. "You were talking to me on the phone and all I could think of was that Joan Baez song we used to sing, all of us hanging around smoking pot and thinking we were hippies or something." She sings a bit of it, about ghosts and voices on the telephone, her voice contralto and pure. It makes him hurt inside to hear her sing.

She stops singing in the middle of a line and grins at him. "We were sure melancholy little shits, weren't we? Seventeen and bleeding all over the place. Like we'd ever really had much of a chance to suffer about anything yet."

"No, maybe not." He blows out his breath in a sigh. He rinses out a cup but doesn't turn around. "But we thought we did. I guess we have one hell of a perspective on that now."

"I guess we do," she says, and she starts singing again and he closes his eyes and listens and all around him the world seems to shift ever so slightly, falling away in a steady rain of dust, all at the speed of light.

★

It is Saturday, Jack's day with Jay. He remembers about the dog the instant the front door has closed behind the boy. Jay is looking around wondering where his dog is. The boy starts for the garage door and Jack stops him and tells him about Hoover running away. He tells him what the cop said about the pound and Jay nods as if he understands what the cop had meant.

"I've seen them before," he says, "catching other dogs around here. They won't put him to sleep, will they?"

"No, not a chance. They'll just give him a place to bed down and something to eat until we get there to pick him up. It'll be fine." He put his hand on his son's shoulder to try to be reassuring, but that feels strange, he thinks, to both of them. "Have you had breakfast yet?" Jack asks.

Jay nods. "At the IHOP. Can we go get Hoover now?"

"Sure," Jack tells him. "Just let me get my shoes on."

At the pound a pleasant-looking, thin woman peers at them over her glasses from behind the counter. She's mid-thirtyish, Jack judges, her hair already tinged the slightest bit with gray.

"Missing dog," Jack says. "A beagle-basset hound mix, about yea-high." He holds a hand flat about a foot over the counter to show her. "I called earlier, talked to some kid who said he didn't know if the dog was here, and wouldn't go back and look, so we came on down to see for ourselves."

"Yeah, that would be Irwin. He's kind of a wanker, but he comes in when he says he will, so we can't complain too much. Most everyone's a volunteer here. I come in sometimes on weekends, mostly on Sundays, though. I'm Tammy. Hi."

"Hi," he says.

"What's your dog's name?" she asks Jay.

"Hoover. Like a vacuum. He's never run away before. I don't think he has. He's pretty good, most of the time."

"Well, all of us mess up from time to time. Let's go see if we can track him down, give him a pardon and all."

She lifts up a hinged piece of the counter to let them through and they follow her back to the kennels. The hallway leading back heavy is with the smell of urine. Dogs bark and whine in chorus as they hear them coming. Jay presses up close to Jack and Jack is so grateful for the spontaneous contact that he catches himself smoothing the boy's hair down with his hand, the way Lucy does sometimes.

Tammy talks to them over her shoulder. "We usually keep a list of who we've got staying here, but some people didn't show last night, so nobody filled in the breeds like they should have when the dogs were brought in. Things get a little disorganized around here, but we eventually sort it out."

She walks up and down the aisles with Jack and Jay in tow, peering into concrete and chain-link runs made shadowy and dim by the little, bright-hot squares of light coming through the dog doors. A lot of the dogs look old and very tired and like they are suffering in the heat. Very few of them look as if anyone might want to rescue them from this and give them a home.

They find Hoover in the last run on the third aisle. He has heard or smelled them coming and is running in tight little circles inside his cage, bumping up against the chain-link, barking and whining.

"There he is," Jay announces. He waits patiently while Tammy undoes the latch and lets Hoover out. Hoover leaps up on him and bounces off, then jumps at Jack, pawing his jeans. Tammy puts a leash on him, a braided thing that passes through itself like a lasso, and hands it to Jay. "Just until we get him to your car, hon," she tells him. Jay takes it and they follow Tammy back up front, Hoover straining at the leash and Jay pulling him back to heel like Jack has taught him. Hoover isn't having any of that; this is all too much for him.

Back at the counter, Tammy hoists herself up on the tall stool and they stand beside her while she fills out papers. Jay is very patient, very solemn, watching her.

"Ol' Hoover's sure a lucky boy. Already got his tags and everything. We would've looked that license up and called if you hadn't come down. And he doesn't look much worse for the wear, does he? I'd treat him for fleas when you get him home, though—he's probably just crawling with them." She speaks to them both while she writes, the fountain pen she is using making a dry and rapid scratching, like the sound of mice in the walls at night. She taps at a place on the form with the pen. "Sign here and you can take the runaway home." Jack takes the pen, signs, and hands it back to her.

"Thank you," she says. "There's usually twenty-five bucks connected with this transaction, but we'll just let Hoover slide this time. What do you say, chief?"

This last she directs at Jay. "Sure," he says. "That's great. Isn't it, Dad?"

"It is," he tells her. "I appreciate it a lot."

"Don't mention it. I got a soft spot for people who act responsible about their dogs."

He feels a little twinge at that. Even with Hoover, he's been walking the thin edge of honest responsibility for a good, long while. But she is right that the dog doesn't look any worse for the wear. He's eating up all the attention he's getting from Jay now, nipping at the boy's face and squirming around on the concrete floor in an abandoned little ecstasy of love.

"Now that's a happy puppy," Tammy says.

Jay looks up and she smiles at him. The sweat glimmers alongside her nose like tears. Jack is struck by an impulse. "Hey, look," he says.

She looks at him. Jay does, too. "Look," he says again, feeling strange, feeling a little numbness suddenly just above the hinges of his jaw. He's thinking, Do I really want to say this? What the hell, he thinks. What the hell. "Would you like to go out? Tonight?"

She closes one eye and cocks her head a bit. "Out? Me? Uh, like we just met. Maybe I'm married, you know." She holds up her left hand so they can both look at it. "Well, I guess not. Pretty sudden, though."

Jack rubs his forehead with the heel of his hand. "Yeah. I don't know where that came from. Sorry."

She tilts her head and smiles at him. "I don't know. I might like that." She moves the smile over to Jay. "Both of you going?"

"I don't know," Jay says. He looks a little stunned.

"Sure he can," Jack says, "Hell, Hoover too."

"Well, then," she says, "that'd be OK."

★

Darien's car is in the driveway when they pull up, and he sees her standing in the doorway, waiting for them to get out of the car. She gestures from the doorway. "I let myself in. Come on inside, both of you. There's something I want you to look at."

"Jeez!" Jay says when they're inside.

Jack knows what he means. The living room is spotless, every stack of newspaper, every dish and beer can gone. The air is heavy with the lemony smell of furniture polish

"Voila," Darien says. She does a Vanna White sort of flourish, one yellow-gloved hand on her hip, the other sweeping the room.

"Wow," Jay says, "what does the kitchen look like?" He skips into the kitchen. "Wow," he says again through the partition.

"Christ, Darien. Do you do this for every client who gives you a key? Now I really do feel like a pig."

"If the curly tail fits, Wilbur. You can't sell a messy house, first rule of the trade. Or second. I think 'lie like a Republican' is the first. I've been digging through your shit for two hours." She throws a rubber glove at him playfully.

Hoover darts over to wrap himself around her ankles, then deserts her just as quickly to bounce himself against Jack's knees.

"Get the dog, will you," Jack asks Jay. He gathers Hoover up, spilling some soda on the carpet to do it, and carries him squirming back to his room.

Darien picks up the glove she threw at him. "I've still got a bathroom to see to. See if you can entertain yourself without making a mess." She follows Jay into the back of the house.

When she is out of sight he drops onto the couch. "I've got plans this evening," he says then, loud enough so she can hear.

"You do?" she asks, coming back into the room.

"Yeah. In a little while I do. A date, sort of. Not really, though."

"Sure," she says, "know all about 'em. Who's the lucky girl?"

"Somebody I met at the pound. Picking up the dog. We just talked, you know." He can't quite understand why he's telling her all this. Why he feels the need.

He can see that she's considering. "OK. No sweat. What about Jay?"

"He's coming, too."

"On a date. You know, kids don't generally do that. Could screw him up for life, seeing his ol' dad on the make." She laughs, starts to put her hand to her face, to touch her own cheek, then realizes that she's still wearing the yellow rubber gloves and lets the hand drop again. "Look, I'll watch him. No problem."

"I couldn't let you do that," he says.

"Sure you could. Jay likes me, don't you think? And it'll give me a chance to get at some things I kind of skipped over 'cause I was busy using a bulldozer to get the mess out of that kitchen."

"Well, what the hell," Jack says, "if you don't mind."

"Not at all." She stands looking at him for a long moment, then takes in a deep breath. "Guess I'll go finish the toilet, then." She turns around and leaves again. He can hear water start running in the back. Well, he thinks to himself, that was damned unpleasant. He sits for about ten minutes, then wanders back. Darien is in the guest bathroom as he goes by, on her hands and knees, ministering to the tub. She half-smiles, half-grimaces at him. Jay is in his room, headphones on. Jack waves a hand at him to get his attention.

"Yeah, Dad?" he says, pulling one side of the headphones back behind his ear.

"Where's Hoover?"

"Under the bed. Chewing on his rawhide thing. He's a happy puppy."

"I've heard." He closes one eye and tilts his head back, looking at Jay along the plane of his nose. It's an old signal he knows Jay will recognize. It means "'fess up, no bullshit, I can take it."

"Darien said she'd stay with you. You going to be all right here?"

"Yeah, sure. I'll be fine."

108

"OK," Jack says. He feels like he ought to say something more but he can't think of anything that matters much. "I'm going to get cleaned up and go pick up Tammy. I won't be gone too long. Promise."

"OK." He touches the headphones with a forefinger, as if in preparation for pushing them back over his ears, meaning *I understand, go ahead and get on with it.*

"All right."

Jack goes into his room and finds a clean shirt and some slacks in the closet. He showers, standing so that the water rushes over his face and ears in a numbing roar of white noise. He feels very odd, very disconnected from the people around him, scattered among the rooms of his house, his son, his old dope-smoking buddy Darien. These people care about him and wish him well, but it is hard to really feel that. He doesn't feel particularly needy. He's managing—in a rather shitty way, maybe, but managing. He's spent a lot of years taking care of himself, keeping his family fed, covering his ass and theirs.

The worst of it is—and he is a little surprised to realize this, standing blind and deaf under the hot water pouring out of the showerhead— how little he really feels about it one way or another. A little affection, maybe, for these particular people. A little irritation. Once in a while he sees something in Jay that blindsides him, but he has trouble reaching even the residue of that at the moment. He loves his son; he can say that, but usually what he feels is something dry and practical, responsibility, maybe a little guilt.

And friendship is something even less tangible than that. There are never any real friendships anymore, not the kind you'd see on old movies where two people, even men, can care so much that it tears them up inside when they, inevitably, find some way to hurt each other.

There are acquaintances full of polite distance and there are old friends who aren't really friends because they aren't truly real in a way, because they can't be who you remember them to be, because those people are only ghosts made up of idealizations and the sticky sentimentality of nostalgia. You can only be disappointed, either way.

He could go out there now and talk over old times with Darien, maybe even give her a tumble later if that's what she wants, and not really feel a damned thing. A little regret maybe, a sad little swelling of lust between old and faithful friends. Poor pitiful Jack. Crap, he tells himself. Try and act like a man, Jackie-boy. He laughs a little at that, and turns off the water.

In the echoey, drippy quiet he can hear Darien in the other bathroom, singing to herself. It is like something you might hear in a canyon somewhere off in a desert, the sound faraway and out of place and so tenderly beautiful it can break your heart if you're unwary enough to listen.

★

The date is uneventful, Greek food, a movie where he puts his hand on Tammy's thigh in the dark and feels her knees part and then he can't make himself press on, just leaves his hand there like something he's forgotten until the movie's over and he takes her home and she looks at him, disappointed, and gives him a dry kiss goodnight.

When he gets home, he pulls the car into the garage and lets it run there for a few minutes, thinking, then he shuts it off and closes the garage door. Darien is sitting on the couch when he walks in, watching the news.

"How was everything?" she asks.

"Fine. You know. A movie. People got married, I think. Happily every after and all that."

"Hey, sorry I asked," she says, but her voice is playful. She starts to get up and he motions her to stay.

In the house they sit on the couch with the TV on and talk, sitting close. It feels awkward and too intimate but Jack drinks his beer and tells himself to loosen up and try to enjoy the company.

"You know," Darien tells him, "I'm still not sure why you called me in the first place."

"I got a house to sell."

"I'm willing to bet there are at least six hundred licensed real estate agents in Orange County. Probably more. Other than me, I mean."

"Yeah, well, I knew I could trust you. You know what they say about lawyers and people who sell real estate."

"No," she says, faking disbelief, "what do they say?"

He gives her a look. "Besides, I wondered. About you, what had happened."

"You mean, like whether I'd puffed out like a heifer, lost my teeth, that sort of thing?"

"Something like that. Whether your life was good."

"It's great," she says. She looks at him hard, like she is trying to tell him something with her eyes and he is just not getting it. "Top notch. Now you know."

"Ah," Jack says. He decides to concentrate on what's on TV. "I hate that guy," he says. David Letterman is on the screen, talking to Connie Chung.

He scoops the remote up from the coffee table and flips around a bit and passes something that looks interesting and flips back to it. A late-night televangelist sits behind a desk in a dust brown suit, looking a lot like an overly animated Johnny Carson, with a painting of a city skyline filling the background behind him. Jack touches up the sound a little. He's making promises and asking for pledges, squeezing his eyes shut and trembling with the intensity of it all. "You should always give God your best!" he shouts. His face is shiny with sweat and he looks like he's in pain, shot through with sincerity and need. He says, "You say to yourself, 'I'd like to move to the other side of town'—well, God wants you to move to the other side of town." He speaks rapidly without pauses, mostly asking for vows, declaring "there's a woman in Titusville, a woman who is troubled in her heart about a loveless marriage—God wants her to make a two hundred-dollar vow, God wants her to receive happiness, praise Jesus!"

"Oh, Lordy," Darien says. "What a hoot. I didn't know guys like that still existed."

"The wonders of cable," Jack says. The television preacher is leaning forward now, toward the camera. He looks like he's about to weep, just barely holding it in. "There's a widow out there," he moans, "who needs to get herself right with Jesus—God loves you when you're all alone, God watches over the little widows." That's me, Jack thinks, a little widow. He looks at the guy and he knows he must be worth millions, vows pouring in every night, tearstained checks from the faithful and the lonely. But Jack, too, wants God to love him. He wants the man in the dust-colored suit to weep for him.

"Can we turn this now?" Darien says. She takes the remote from Jack's hand and jumps it rapid-fire across a dozen channels. She stops on a movie with Dustin Hoffman in it, dressed like an Indian brave. He's sitting in a teepee, talking to Chief Dan George about hating white men. After a couple of minutes, a commercial comes on for a 1-900 number. "Have a confidential affair," the oriental woman on the screen croons.

"There you go," Jack says. "Who needs real women?"

"Oh, stuff it," Darien tells him.

They watch the movie, Hoffman trying to get revenge on General Custer. Darien leans in against Jack and puts her head on his chest. After a while he puts his arm around her shoulder, his hand on her arm just below her elbow. She puts a hand flat against his stomach. It feels natural and comfortable, nothing sexual. The whole room seems filled with something he can't define. His heart aches a little, in a self-conscious way.

The movie ends and he can feel Darien breathing deeply and evenly against him, her eyes closed. The skin across her cheeks is smooth and flawless but even in the jumpy blue light from the TV he can see the small lines in the corner of her eyes. Her boy-short hair looks glossy in the TV light, perfectly straight, tapering sharply to her thin neck. The air-conditioning kicks on with a puff of air that stirs the tiny, fine blond hairs in the hollow behind and below her ear. He leans his head down and kisses her there, tasting the smooth, flat dryness of her skin.

"Um," she says. She looks up at him again without saying anything more. For a long moment he just looks back at her, into those eyes that he remembers now, from before, when they were both seventeen and her eyes were this same lucent blue. His hand moves behind her head and he kisses her again, on the mouth, and lingers there while she kisses him back.

Then they stop. She looks at him and her face is red and flushed but she's smiling, a little embarrassed maybe. "Nice," she says.

"Very," he says, and he means it, but he has a little trouble meeting her eyes.

"This seems kind of familiar, doesn't it?"

"Kind of." He thinks about kissing her again, and then doesn't. They hover in an odd kind of equilibrium for the space of two breaths, then she sits up and sighs and he takes a deep breath too, and the moment seems over, though he's not sure enough of that to say anything yet. There's a warm spot in the middle of his chest from the heat of her face and he puts his hand over it absentmindedly, as if to hold it there.

"I'm sorry," he says then, though he's not sure exactly why he feels the need to apologize. It just feels like it needs to be said.

"It's all right." Her voice is very quiet and he wonders if he's offended her. She picks up her purse from the floor beside the chair, then comes over and kisses him but not in the same way; this is sincere but quick and spiceless. "Gotta go. Got a closing in the morning." She touches him on the cheek with a fingertip and goes to the door. He follows her out.

The crickets and the cicadas are going and it seems loud, the air full of a throbbing underbeat like the way music feels through a brick wall, all bass and vibration. Darien gets into her car and rolls the window down and Jack comes up close.

"Well, goodnight," Jack says.

"It was," she says. "I missed you."

"I missed you, too."

"No you didn't. Not much, anyway. But maybe you would've if you'd thought about it."

She reaches up and grabs his ear between her thumb and forefinger and pulls him close. She kisses him again, quick but this time genuine, heartfelt, like a promise.

Then she puts the car into gear and he steps back. She backs out into the street and taps the horn once so that it lets out a mild little bleat and then she accelerates away down the street and is gone.

The concrete is cold under his bare feet and feels sandpapery and unpleasant. He stands there looking at the neighborhood. He thinks about Darien and realizes he doesn't feel very good; in fact he feels lousy, a kind of punky, dragging malaise starting to soak inward through his skin toward his heart and bones. Ah, shit, he thinks. Ah, shit.

A bug-zapper pops somewhere near, a loud report and sizzle. "Jesus," he says aloud. "Must've been big as a pigeon."

He looks around for the zapper's purple-blue glow and thinks he sees it on one corner of Noah's house, but the light moves when he turns his head and he realizes it's just some sort of afterimage he hadn't noticed until he concentrated, some fuzzy blue something left on his retina by the TV or by Darien's headlights. He closes his eyes tightly but the color sticks.

Might've been a bat, he thinks. Trying to grab an easy meal, what with all those bugs. Somebody should have told him about free lunches. Now that he's aware of it, the blue cloud of light hovers persistently in front of him, superimposed over the night sky. He feels somehow even lousier, haunted by a little blue ghost that he feels the itching need to reach out and pluck as it bobs across the landscape everywhere he looks. His own sad little poltergeist.

★

Darien rings the doorbell at five P.M. on the nose. She's wearing her real estate outfit and kisses him on the cheek in a businesslike way. A couple has made an offer on the house, a few thousand lower than he'd been asking. They're young people, she tells him, with a new baby, and they don't have much down, so they're trying to qualify for an FHA loan.

"Do it," he tells Darien, and she shows him where to sign, tells him she talked the couple out of trying to get him to carry the points on their loan for them. He tells her he's appreciative. Then it's done and she stands up to go.

"So, Jack," she says, "are you going to be all right with this?"

"Sure. I'll manage," he says, but he feels bad and he's not sure why. He's thought about losing the house for months. But this is more real. He'll have to find somewhere else to live now, and he feels a sudden, deep inertia tug him down. Too much effort, too much adjustment.

Darien sits back down at the table and looks him in the eye. "Why don't you let me buy you a drink? Kind of celebrate."

He looks at her and knows she's trying to help. "I'd like that," he tells her. "I think that'd be good."

"Well, then," she says.

They go to a sports bar out on Colonial Boulevard. The place is called The Draft Pick and is pretty empty when they get there, though all ten big-screen TVs are on, most of them showing the same basketball game. They sit at the bar, where there's only a small TV, and order drinks. It's happy hour and the bartender pours them doubles.

Darien loosens up some, takes off her blazer and faces him, her knees against his left thigh where they sit on the barstools.

"Well," she says, "How's it feel to have one load off, anyway?"

"Queen for the Day. I could dance in little circles for joy."

"Ha. I'll bet." She takes a drink of her gin and tonic and looks at him sideways with one eye. "You're not being a wiseass to cover up on me again, are you? I mean, I know you're big into this real-men-don't-show-their-feelings bullshit."

"I'll live." She gives him a look. "Seriously, it's all a load off my mind. I'm grateful. One happy camper." He gives her a goofy grin to show her. She slaps him on the arm.

They finish their drinks and the bartender brings them more. He pours with a flourish, happy to have some customers, Jack supposes, and fills the glasses until they're brimming. Some of Jack's slops out onto the bar when he tries to pick the glass up. "My cup runneth over," he says. "How can I not be happy?"

Halfway through the second gin and tonic, Darien's eyes soften up. She stops looking at him as though he were a horse she'd had to shoot, for which he's grateful.

"You know," she tells him, "I'm pretty pissed you still haven't asked me why I'm not married."

He shrugs. "None of my business, I thought."

"Why not? I got no secrets. Go ahead. Ask me."

"So why?"

"Maybe I don't like men."

"Meaning?"

"What do you mean 'meaning'? You don't understand the phrasing? You need a map? Some directions?"

He takes a drink, then holds the glass up and looks at her through it. "So. You prefer the ladies?"

She waits five or ten seconds before saying anything. She sighs. "No. I mostly prefer men still. At least for certain, mostly mechanical, sorts of functions. Just trying to get a rise out of you, Jackie-boy. Didn't work, though, did it?"

"Guess not."

"Not that I haven't considered it. I mean, women are cleaner, for one thing. More responsible. More dependable. But then again, they borrow your clothes. And I like the chivalry stuff, defending my honor and all that. Opening doors. You know." She looks thoughtful, finishes her drink. "No, on the whole, I still prefer men. Somewhat."

"We're all pretty relieved."

"I'll bet you are. So you want to know why?"

"Tell me."

She leans in close and whispers. "Nobody—and I mean not one mother's son—has asked me. Surprised?"

"Yeah, I am," he says sincerely. "Very."

"Why? Because I'm so knock-down gorgeous?"

She isn't gorgeous. She sits on the stool across from him and she is small and thin and pretty, but not beautiful. Not striking. What she looks is wholesome, he thinks. A little masculine, maybe. Safe. Comfortable to be with, but not exciting. "Because you're a hell of a sweet person," he tells her. "Because you're kind and caring and honest."

"Gee, thanks. I was hoping you'd back me up on the gorgeous thing. Sweet's good, I guess. It's an asset, something you can bargain with."

She seems suddenly shy, won't look him in the eyes. "I thought I was close a couple of times, you know, a few years back. A couple of guys who seemed compatible, treated me well. Stuck around. They just didn't fall in love with me. Maybe because I didn't fall in love with them. I'm pretty practical in a lot of ways, but not in that way. If I don't love somebody, I don't think I can hide it. Things always got to feeling kind of stiff. Formal, I guess. Uncommitted. Anyhow, they went elsewhere to throw out the ol' nuptial anchor. Left little ol' me adrift in a sea of eminent spinsterhood." She sighs again. "God, I'm depressing myself."

"Lord, Darien. The way I remember it, you never did give much of a damn about men. Boys. The tough girl with the guitar and the joint hanging off her lip. All attitude. Fuck 'em all. Hell, you might well have been gay for all I knew."

She suddenly looks as if she might cry. "Oh, thanks. Thanks a lot. Fucking little you knew. Fucking little." She takes a deep, angry pull on her drink and he realizes she is crying, just a little. "Damned liquor makes me weepy," she says. She puts the drink down and uses her cocktail napkin to rub at her eyes. "Shit," she says.

"Hell," he says, feeling dumb.

"Oh, it's not your fault. What the hell did we know? Look at you—you fall for some red-haired cheerleader type and bingo, eighteen years old and Jack's goin' to the chapel, and then you're gone. I cried for you for a week. I thought you'd ruined your life with some damn bimbo who was going to break your heart. Oh, man, I ate it up. I was dying for some tragedy. Or at least some irony. Small towns are so damned boring."

"I aim to please."

She looks thoughtful again. "Yeah, you do. You always did. That's about half your problem. You're too goddamned nice, in a selfish sort of way."

He tries not to feel hurt. "Now, what the hell is that supposed to mean?"

"All you southern boys are the same, you know that? And it doesn't matter if you come from trash or you come from blue blood, river-bottom planter, it's all the same. It's something in the water, I think, or in all that greasy shit they fed us when we were kids. Men should act this certain way, is what's on top of it, but underneath it is this little boy crap that takes all the spine out of that chivalry and honor shit and makes it hollow. Like a big fucking, rotten oak tree. I hope it falls on your goddamned heads."

"Jesus, Darien."

"And what makes it worse is women're no damned better. We're not one ounce more honest, and we buy into the same load of crap. By rights, every damn one of us should spend her life in crinoline, just waiting for a chance to pull off a swoon. God, look at me. I can't let that shit go, either. Give me a man with manners who says 'ma'am' and expects nothing more than to sire the new Sons of the Confederacy on my lily-white form so his great and honorable line will continue on unbroken. And if I can't find that fine figure of a gentleman, why honey, I gots to pull myself up and get crusty. Us southern spinsters got spunk, we'll spit in a man's eye soon as look at him. All you got to do is watch *Designing Women* reruns to know that. So far, I'm only half-crusty, though. No tougher than shoe leather." She sighs again, winding down. "I wish I was from New England. At least there all they expect is that you wear white and write poetry. Seems peaceful. Look at Emily Dickinson."

"Well, I had a professor once, said she might have been gay."

"Oh, thanks."

"Don't mention it."

"Asshole."

"So I've been told." He's not entirely sure she means all this, or where she means to take it. Just let it flow, he thinks. See what happens. They both pretend to watch the basketball game for a while.

A commercial comes up on the TV. Darien finishes her drink and sets the glass carefully down on the bar.

"I don't feel as sorry for myself as I sound," she says. "I just feel kind of lousy right now. The last few years or so, I've been doing OK with it all. And then you came along. Bang, out of nowhere, came the phone call. That rusty old voice from the past. And what did he want? Wanted me to sell his goddamned house, is what he wanted."

"Hey—" he begins, and she lays one hand on his forearm and leans in close again.

"Don't worry about it, Jack. I told you, I'm into irony. I can deal with it."

"Well, good," he says lamely.

She pats his arm. The bartender drifts by and smiles at them. "Get you folks anything else?" he asks.

"Uh-uh," Darien tells him. She looks at Jack.

"No," he says, and Darien pats his arm again. "I think we're going home now."

★

He wakes up at about midnight to the sound of rain plinking on the tin cap the contractor had put on the chimney to keep birds and squirrels out.

He eases out of the bed to keep from waking Darien, who is buried somewhere beneath the covers, her head tucked under the comforter, nested like a hamster.

There had been a little more crying when they'd gotten back to his house. They'd watched TV for a while, just holding each other and not talking, getting comfortable with the idea. Later, they made love. Nothing urgent. Old friends fooling around.

The house is quiet beneath the sound of the rain and the far-off rumble of thunder. Hoover looks up from his bed when he walks by, thumps his tail like a gavel against the floor, happy for the company.

He gets a beer from the refrigerator and goes back into the living room. He leaves the lights off and watches the rain for a while, watching the way it streaks the window, making the streetlights look jagged and weary.

Darien touches his shoulder and he jumps, startled. She puts her arms around his waist and he turns around and hugs her back, pressing her close. Her bare skin is warm and dry and she looks up at him, her eyelids droopy with sleep. "What are you watching?" she asks.

"The world out there, getting washed."

She leans out a bit from him to look, her breast squashing against his upper arm. "Pretty wet, all right." She watches for a while and then yawns. "Sleepy," she says.

He bends over and puts his forearm behind her knees and scoops her up into his arms.

"Hey!" she says, and puts her arms around his neck. She snuggles her head against his shoulder and he stands there with her a while, holding her like a baby. "Nice," she whispers. She's light and soft and the smell of her is soft, too, clean and sweet. It starts to rain harder outside and the streetlights go really sloppy, dim and abstract through the water pouring in tattered sheets off the eaves, and he can't understand why seeing that makes his heart seem to shake and sputter inside his chest as if it wants to quit him just for the spite of everything it can't accept.

★

Darien falls gently back to sleep. Jack lies listening to the rainwater thumping through the gutterspouts, listens to it slow and finally almost stop so that there's only the dripping and the sound of thunder. Sleep won't come. So he eases out of bed and Darien stirs but doesn't wake. The house feels small and breathless and he thinks maybe he'll go for a walk, then thinks of the rain and decides he won't, then changes his mind again. He puts on shorts and running shoes and goes outside. Everything is dark and foggy and he starts jogging down the wet, steamy pavement of the street, though he hasn't run in weeks and he can feel how out of shape he's gotten. It feels good outside, alone, underneath a lowering sky orange with the reflected light of the city.

He goes only about two blocks from the house when he sees lights come around a corner a few blocks ahead and sees enough of the car in the streetlight glow that he can tell it's a police cruiser. He turns up a side street almost without thinking about it and picks up his pace. A few moments later he hears the sizzle of the cruiser's tires as it comes around the corner behind him and he cuts out across a yard toward an opening between two houses. The cruiser's blue lights flash on and an amplified voice crackles at him to stop.

He keeps running, though he knows it's stupid, that he's asking for real trouble. But the thought of having to stand in the wet suburban street and explain himself to a suspicious cop just seems more than he can bear. He darts between the houses and goes over a fence into someone's backyard, and then over another fence and into an alley. He sees the blue lights flickering in the trees behind him, and he turns left onto another road, cuts across more yards, and dives at a dead run into a stretch of brushy woods that borders the subdivision. He pushes himself through palmetto and thorny vines. He can see the highway ahead, a few late cars sliding by and disappearing under an overpass. There's a low fence beside the right-of-way and he vaults it and runs alongside the highway, heading south. A car passes him doing sixty or seventy, blowing its horn and spraying him with dirty water from the pavement. His breath is coming hard now, and he's thinking *just go home*, but one foot keeps falling in front of the other and he keeps going, into the underpass and down the road that runs away ahead. He's wet and terrified and lost somewhere between coldness and exhaustion, but he keeps on. His whole body holds him in a painful grip and with each step a phrase repeats itself in a foolish rhythm inside his head: *happy puppy, happy puppy.* But underneath it all he can feel something else in the tightening and loosening of his muscles, in the cramp building under the ribs on his left side, unbearable as desperation: the grief of trying too hard as always, running though there's nowhere to go, trying the only way he can to learn how to stop.

JULIA LOVING THE
FACE OF GOD

★━━━━━★━━━━━★

Julia Ross learned to live with a certain spartan simplicity in the months after her oldest son died. It became her way of balancing out her husband's excesses, by answering them with her own passive resistance to the elaborate, the ornate, and the careless. The first things she removed from her life were the indulgences of expectation and grief. Far easier to live in the calm acceptance of things as they were. She started going to church again, though her people had never been much for church going. When she was a girl, they'd only gone on Easter and Christmas, but she'd always known that that paucity was more her father's doing than her mother's wish. Most people went to church, she knew, to encourage their own good fortune by displaying to God and to the world their faithfulness. But Julia didn't want anything; she went to pay penance and to remind herself how insignificant her own sacrifices really were in the face of God's grace and Christ's passion.

Walker, her husband, detested the church on principle, and that, too, was an incentive. She prayed for his soul on Sundays but it was her one secret and unconfessed vanity that she knew beyond all doubt that any prayer where Walker was concerned was seed sown on barren ground.

Walker Ross was bound for hell and she took a modestly sinful satisfaction in the knowledge of that certainty.

Her family had always been Methodist, and Walker's people were hard-shell Southern Baptists, but Julia had tried several different brands of worship and had settled in finally with the Holiness Church of God. It had been a long journey of trial and error, finding the venue for her faith. She'd even spent a month attending mass and had found with the Catholics a good and severe sense of order and priority, far better than the skimmed-over and milk-weak variety of worship followed by the Methodists and Lutherans. On the whole, though, the Catholics had seemed a little weary of themselves to her, a little too perfunctory in their observances. And there was the fact, of course, that they were idolatrists.

The Presbyterians had held her for almost a year until she began to find unbearable the gray patience of the retired northerners who made up most of the congregation, the yellow smell of their age, the sun-bleached body of Christ upon which they worshipped in flesh worn through like the thin promise of redemption, believing mostly in everything they had lost or left behind. Their patience she could understand, but not the irony of their faith. Everything she lived was irony. From her church, she wanted the Holy Spirit, undiluted and untempered, direct as a hammer.

The Holiness Church of God hammered. It rattled and hummed and praised. It gave her courage and resolve. It made her realize the abiding sanctity of her life as it was, unadorned and humble. It made her forgive Walker for everything he was and almost everything he'd done. So she was as surprised as anyone when she shot him on a calm Sunday afternoon with his own .22 High Standard revolver. It was a beautiful day, very cool for an April in Mascotte Grove, the sky very clear and Walker on the porch drinking Canadian Club and Coke. She was sitting alone in the room behind the porch that her mother had used as a parlor, looking at the blank screen of the television Walker had installed less than a week after her mother's death. She was thinking about God and his judgment and she heard Walker singing, which was something he did sometimes when he was drinking, not loudly, just to himself, out on the porch.

Mona Lisa, Mona Lisa, men have named you, he was singing, *woman with the mysterious smile.*

Calmly—very calmly, she would remember, without the slightest trace of rancor—she stood up from the chair and walked through the hall and up the stairs to Walker's bedroom. She wasn't even sure why; it was as if she were just going along with something her body had decided to do without her. Later she would think about spiritual possession. That very morning she'd been taken by the Holy Spirit and sent shaking and speaking in tongues up the center aisle of the sanctuary. God himself had lain her down hard on the floor in front of the pulpit and possessed her so completely that she wasn't half-aware of what was happening to her, what she was saying, what she was doing.

It was something like that, but much calmer and much more collected. She was moved by a resolve she could swear wasn't her own. She went to the chifforobe that used to belong to her father and opened the doors and took down the pistol from the top shelf. She checked the load, opened up the little cylinder gate and turned the cylinder so that the bright, flat bottom of each shell clicked by. She closed the gate and went out the door and down the stairs.

Walker was leaning one shoulder against a porch column. He looked over his other shoulder at her as the screen door creaked and she realized he was urinating off the porch into the azaleas. She waited until he zipped himself up and turned to face her, then she raised the pistol, cocked it, aimed, and fired. All without the slightest volition on her own part, she would swear. She stood apart and watched it happen, though not without a twinge of satisfaction, she would have been the first to admit, if anyone had asked her.

Walker went down with a howl. He lay on the porch and writhed, as if, she thought, he too was possessed by the Spirit. She went back inside the house and put the pistol down on the sideboard in the dining room, then went into the kitchen where the phone was and called the sheriff's office and told the woman who answered the phone that she'd shot her husband.

"Is he dead?" the woman wanted to know.

"Not likely," Julia told her. Then she went back into the parlor and sat down in front of the TV and waited for them to come.

★

The sheriff was a large man, red faced and expansive in his khaki uniform, silver star glowing on his barrel chest like an icon. He was standing in the high school principal's office when Fisher walked in, looking into a glass case filled with trophies won by the various sports teams. "Hey, Fisher," he said, his voice basso profundo and sad.

"Hello, Mr. Parks," Fisher said. Fisher was a little nervous, though he hadn't done anything that he could think of to get him in serious trouble.

But the sheriff shook his head and looked sad and put his hand on Fisher's shoulder, not like he was going to drag him in, but like he was trying to hold him steady, and he told him that his momma had shot his daddy, that his daddy was in the county hospital in fairly good condition with a bullet in his upper thigh, and that his momma was sitting in the county lockup.

"Her bail'll be set in the morning, son. I think you ought to be there to take her home. Give her some support." He didn't say anything about giving his daddy support.

"OK," Fisher told him, thought he didn't have any real idea of how he was going to manage it, where to get the money, or what to say to his mother after she'd shot his father.

Sheriff Parks squeezed his shoulder. He leaned in close and Fisher could smell the beer on his breath. "You come on down there, son, and we'll take care of it. It's not the end of the world. Your momma's a fine woman, just pushed a little too far."

"OK," Fisher said again, though for all he knew the sheriff was dead wrong and the end of the world itself could indeed be at hand, his mother's performance just the first insane spark that would ignite the conflagration. It felt that way, though only for a moment. Then it felt

125

another way entirely. It felt inevitable. It even felt like God's justice, which was strange, Fisher thought, since, like his father, he'd long ago stopped believing in such things.

★

Fisher sat through three bail hearings before his mother's name came up. He expected her to look like the others had looked, ragged and tired, faces pale and a little scared, but she didn't. She looked, he thought, like a righteous angel of God. She was wearing black, widow's weeds, he thought, though really it was just her Sunday dress. Her face was smooth and unworried and when she came into the room she gave the justice of the peace a look that Fisher could only think of as smug. No tears, but he hadn't expected there to be any. Julia was ramrod straight with fortitude and probity. She was so busy being untouched by what was going on, Fisher thought, she hadn't even bothered to notice her own son sitting there watching.

Someone must have told the sheriff that it was Julia Ross's turn, because he came into the little hearing room and lumbered up front and leaned in close and spoke to the justice of the peace for a moment. The justice of the peace peered at Julia under his brows and shook his head.

"What the hell, Harlan? She shot her husband. She admits she shot him. He's sitting down there at the hospital with a hole in his leg and you decide you're not going to charge her? Attempted homicide? Assault? What have you?"

"Husband doesn't want to press the assault. Evidence shows no intent to kill."

The justice of the peace snorted through his nose. "Oh, bullshit, Harlan. She said she shot him, she wrote it down–" He shuffled through the papers in the file, picked one out. "–and she signed it. So it ain't any part of an accident we're talking about."

"Look, maybe it wasn't accidental in the strict sense. But I was with her daddy when he taught her to shoot. She shot where she aimed, Eddy." He looked thoughtful. "Or maybe just an inch or two off to one side."

"Well, I'm not letting this go without at least a disturbing the peace."

"That'll hunt."

"All right, then. Recognizance." He closed the file, handed it off. He glared at Julia. "Mrs. Ross, you are released. Try to keep your hands off of your husband's handguns in the future. The clerk will have some papers for you to sign. Next case."

Julia nodded, stood up, and started out without a word. She saw Fisher and stopped. He expected her to say something to him, an explanation, an apology, but she kept her silence, waited for him to get up out of the folding chair and take her arm and lead her outside to where his best friend Donny was waiting for them, leaning up against his car, trying hard not to smile at the picture of Fisher walking arm in arm with his murderous and completely unrepentant mother out of the county courthouse.

Fisher glared at him and ushered Julia to the car. "Pretty day," Donny said, and Julia squinted at the bright, hot pavement of the courthouse parking lot and up at the glittering Florida sun hung in its empty blue sky and said, "Praise the Lord."

⋆

She loved her remaining son, Julia she was sure she did, loved him terribly, in ways that made her forget herself and the cool distance she'd achieved from the unkempt nature of life in general. But there was comfort in the objectivity her faith lent her. There was security in not acknowledging the preoccupations and transgressions that she knew with awful certainty lay hidden in his blood like the hard dross that had filled her elder son's heart and killed him as surely as the river he'd driven his car into one drunken night. Not because Fisher was Walker Ross's son, had grown up in the shadow of Walker Ross's influence, but because he was male and therefore cursed in a way she no longer cared to countenance.

She sat at her kitchen table with her Bible open—she'd been reading the parable of the prodigal son and looking for guidance—and found herself caught in a strange tension between her misgivings that Fisher spent so much time away from home with dubious companions and her relief that he was home so relatively little. He was too old to control, nearly a man, and that was undeniably a relief. But she felt prickled by guilt, because she knew she'd taken no real responsibility for his soul until now, when it was very likely too late to do anything about it. She contemplated trying to cajole him into attending her church, but she was relatively certain he wouldn't go, and that even if he did he'd see the service as an outsider would see it, as a violently humiliating kind of abasement, rather than as it was, a rite of devotion, a surrender of self.

Troubling, troubling. She could hear the wind pick up in the trees outside, a muted whispering like children talking in another room. Storm coming. When she was young, she'd liked bad weather, would go outside and stand in a downpour just for the heady sensation of abandon it gave her, the feeling that she was at the very edge of something violent and out of control, thunder rumbling, the air spiced with ozone. Gray days were a delicious melancholy spent alone in her room. Now every day was tinged with grayness and a storm was just a storm.

She prayed and considered and decided that a good example would be enough, perhaps, to move Fisher. Not by her, of course, and certainly not by Walker, who was more watchful of late but as unrepentant and unreconstructed as any white-linen colonel; no, Fisher's witness would have to be someone his own age, someone who could appeal to him in ways his mother never could. It was a problem with no solution, though. Young people didn't come to Julia's church, and even if they did, even in the sanctity and candor of the Holy Spirit, she couldn't begin to know how to approach them.

It was time, perhaps, for retrenchment. There were no half measures, she knew, when it came to devotion, and there was no going back to the mild and the lily-soft when one had lain down upon the altar of Christ's own devotion, been gripped in the iron hand of God's love, had admitted His power and endured His voice speaking through the frail vessel of her body in His divine tongues. But she could live the lie for a time if she had to, and she could think of no other way to make plain to her son God's enduring grace.

She thought on all the churches she had sampled before finding her way. The Baptists, while fine enough in their devotion, were loud enough about it, and their congregation was so large that they just might scare Fisher right off. She didn't even really consider the Methodists or the Lutherans or the Catholics. She decided finally on the Presbyterians, because, insipid as they were, on the whole they were less feeble and buried in the repetitious nonsense of ritual than the rest of them. It was a little church; there weren't all that many Presbyterians around Mascotte Grove. And there were young people among the Presbyterians, boys and girls in whom the Holy Spirit moved, even if under unconscionable restraint. And she was almost confident she could make Fisher go. Faith and the hard hand of discipline can move mountains.

She prayed to God and gave thanks for His unseen hand giving guidance to her thoughts and to her actions, all to the glory of His holy name. *I am powerless in Thy will,* she prayed. *Thy will be done,* she prayed, and when a small and uninvited bubble of doubt winnowed suddenly to the surface of her mind, she added piously and without any irony whatsoever, *however mysterious Thy ways.*

★

The first Sunday morning in July Julia finally cajoled and persuaded a sleepy Fisher out of his bed and into a suit for church. Fisher wasn't just tired, he was hung over, but he didn't want his mother to know that, so when she came into his room barking, "Fisher, Fisher, get up! Church this morning!" he didn't just ignore her or grumble an excuse; he actually got up, because it was the quickest and most efficient way to get her to shut up and leave him alone with his headache and the unsteady nausea that was strong enough to make him desperately *want* to throw up, but not quite enough so that he could actually do it.

He dressed slowly, hoping he wouldn't be ready at the moment when his mother simply couldn't wait for him any longer or risk the shame of arriving after the service had begun. Julia was persistent, though, and he saw her walk past his door to check on him so he made a show of hurrying and before he knew it he actually was ready and Julia hustled him downstairs and urged him out the door. Fisher said, "Jesus, Mom," and got into the car.

The Florida sun was already high and bright, and when Julia pulled the car out from under the trees onto the highway, Fisher cringed down and put his face in his hands to try to block the raw pain of it. It was already getting hot and he rolled down his window for some air and it smelled so good, clean and dry, that he put his forearm over his eyes and leaned his head out the window so the wind blew hard into his face and made his cheeks feel numb.

Julia was almost beside herself with anticipation, and she drove faster than she intended to, considerably over the speed limit when she looked, but she didn't let herself feel guilty about it. She knew the authority of her office, and knew as well that even if the law gave no latitude, the Lord would. She meant to have Fisher quickly and efficiently delivered, saved, and baptized, and regretted only the years of blind selfishness that had kept her from it before.

She wasn't able to park quite as close to the sanctuary as she would have liked, but she was gratified, as she pulled into the sandy parking lot, to see that she'd arrived in good time. People were still making their slow and sociable ways inside, friends chatting and children running around underfoot, little boys with their hair wet and slicked back and the girls wearing pretty print dresses and saddle shoes. Julia didn't speak to anyone as she guided Fisher inside.

Fisher was indeed reluctant. He had just managed to find a sort of balance between the pain in his head and the soothing numbness of the wind on his face when the car jounced off the road into the parking lot and he'd banged his chin against the windowsill. He felt sour and irritable and the only thing that kept him from a flat refusal to budge was the heat, which was already gathering inside the car by the time Julia parked it. Outside the car the sunlight reflected up from the brownish sand in hard waves. "Hell's bells," he said, and ignored his mother's withering look of disapproval. He let her take him by the arm and urge him up out of the car. He kept his eyes squeezed to slits against the light and walked with her toward the church and the dark, cool-looking shadow of its doorway. He could tell people were looking at them, these two church-goers making their way inside, one leading the other as if he were blind and halt, but he was too uncomfortable to care very much.

Julia would normally have tried to find a pew near the altar, but she considered and thought it might be better to keep Fisher a little farther back from the steady gaze of the minister. Not that she was ashamed— God himself was her only judge—but she didn't want Fisher to feel over- whelmed. She guided Fisher firmly toward a pew two rows in from the door, walked him to the end nearest the wall, and pulled him down be- side her. He sat and blinked and looked around and she felt she had done all she could be expected to do. Her son was in God's house; the rest was up to the minister—a man too young and too tentative for her tastes— and to divinity itself.

For his part, Fisher was grateful to be sitting finally in a cool, dim, rea- sonably quiet place. His head was spinning a bit and the pew's hard, wooden back was very comforting in its fixed solidity. He leaned his head back against it and kept his eyes closed and let the world revolve slowly around him. Everything was fine until the music started, the church's organist easing into a lilting version of "One Day at a Time, Sweet Jesus" just as he was starting to feel he could keep himself to- gether for the hour he knew it would take to get through the service. Something about the music, the spirited moaning of the organ, made him suddenly very conscious of where he was. He could hear the quick whispering of the hundred or so souls in the pews around him. He could smell, very distinctly, the musty odor of the hymnals and the cold, damp smell of what he imagined was piety and was in fact the carpet that the good ladies of the church had cleaned the morning before. He felt sud- denly, completely ill. Before he could stop it—before he even really knew it was coming—he pitched forward and threw up onto the seat of the pew in front him, what was left of half of a case of Miller High Life tear- ing loose like something vital. His chest cramped and he couldn't get his breath, and then he vomited again, into the aisle.

His mother grasped him by the arm and towed him up out of the pew and toward the door and he threw up one last time on the red car- pet of the narthex and then he was outside in a sudden blast of sunlight. He felt as if he'd been slapped by a huge, hot hand. He screwed his eyes shut and would have fallen to his knees but his mother, made desperately strong by embarrassment, pulled him back up and dragged him along.

She tried to open his door for him, but he pushed her hand away irritably and told her, "I've got it." And then he fumbled at it blindly for a good minute while she strode around the car and let herself in. He peered at the door handle with his eyes pinched shut and even then the sun's glare off the window felt like a shard of glass lanced through his eyes. He finally wrenched the door open and eased in against the hot air billowing out. He felt so dizzy from the heat and the nausea that he put his head between his knees and kept it there while his mother started the car and pulled it out of the parking lot.

"Roll down your window," she ordered, and he did, feeling for the handle without looking up.

"Please," he said, and what he meant was *Jesus, God, whoever, please make it stop spinning. Please* was just all that he could manage to say out loud.

"Don't ask me," his mother told him, "there's nothing I can do for you. Stick your head back out the window if you want."

And so he did. The wind blew hard in his face, Julia speeding again, anger pushing her foot hard on the accelerator. Fisher sucked in great lungfuls of the clean rushing air, the wind buffeting him like a hurricane, blowing him steadily back, eyes closed, to a place somewhere that, he prayed, was calm and cool and quiet. *Please,* he said again, just to himself, the wind sucking the word away somewhere behind him, where in his fervid imagination he saw it loft and settle in the hot air like a strip of red ribbon flown out of his mouth to tangle in the sandspurs strewn like caltrops on the dusty side of the road.

★

The next morning, Julia Ross woke up from a dark and claustrophobic dream so breathlessly anxious that for a few moments she couldn't make herself so much as stir. She couldn't remember the dream, only the apprehension it left behind like a residue in the muscles of her neck and shoulders.

Just a dream, she told herself.

Something had woken her from it, a noise thumping like her heart. She lay in her bed, which had been her mother's bed, and her grand-mother's, and stared down past the comforting rigidity of the rice-carved bedposts to the window, where a bird fluttered and bumped against the glass, trying, it seemed to get into the room with her. The bird, a wren, hovered, its tail feathers twitching side to side like a cat's tail, it wings beating like a hummingbird's. She could see its little black eyes. It hovered a second more and was gone.

"Jesus, my redeemer," she said, and felt better, and then remembered the day before and her heart grew heavy in her chest. "Oh, Lord," she said. She forced herself to sit up and get out of the bed. She concentrated on not thinking too much. She said the words of various hymns to her-self—not singing, of course, just saying them tunelessly to herself while she dressed. It occupied her mind, a steady grumble of her own white noise. It was something she'd begun to do a month or two before, and now it was a habit she fell into without even thinking, which, in part, defeated the whole purpose, since her thoughts rose through her auto-matic recitation of "Rock of Ages" and "Onward, Christian Soldiers" to bother her still.

In the last months, Julia had found many ways to keep herself busy; she'd long ago fired the woman who came every week to clean, and there was always dust, there were always dishes. Still, she had had far too much time to think. And then, as instruction to her piousness, she listened to the voice down inside that always came to whisper to her of her own sins. Her son's death was a product of her own transgressions, and she knew it, knew it like the words to the Twenty-third Psalm or the Apostles' Creed, deep in her heart. Sin, like anything else we indulge in, she reflected, always comes home to roost.

No one else, of course, was up when she went down to the kitchen to start coffee and to fix herself some oatmeal for her breakfast. Fisher had been out late with his friends the night before, and Julia didn't expect him to wake up before it was time to start getting ready to head over to his summer job. Walker, as usual, would remain sonorously deep in his morning stupor until he smelled her cooking his breakfast bacon and grits, which, ever since she'd shot him, he would wait for her to leave on the stove for him.

She sat down to her coffee at the table but couldn't drink it. It seemed sour to her, and too hot, and she didn't feel able to sit still long enough to let it cool, so she poured it down the sink, took her straw hat from on top of the refrigerator and went outside. She intended to work in the garden, pick tomato worms or pull weeds, maybe, but somehow she just couldn't stop in the garden: the boiled-green of the already-wilting tomato plants and the fuzzy prickliness of the okra just seemed too much to bear.

She walked around the house and saw the grass that needed cutting and the paint that had peeled back to bare boards, and that was hard, too. She found herself back by the kitchen door again and she started up the steps and laid her hand on the knob, but couldn't turn it. She could feel the dew from the grass starting to seep through the seams of her shoes. She should cook Walker his breakfast. She should iron her dress and Walker's suit pants. She turned away from the door and walked across the weedy backyard to the gate to the back pasture.

A cow looked up at her from the claw-footed bathtub her father had rescued from the dump and installed as a watering trough, water streaming greenly from its lower lip. When she opened the gate, the cow spooked and spun away from the trough, trotted twenty or thirty feet away, and stood there staring stupidly at her. She hissed at it and waved her arms, but it didn't spook again. It knew who she was now, and wasn't afraid. Out of spite she picked up a stick and threw it at him. The stick bounced off its side with a sound that reminded Julia of thumping a watermelon to see if it was ripe, but the cow looked at down at the stick where it lay in the grass and didn't move.

"Fine," Julia said aloud, "I surely don't care." She looked back at the house, then back out into the pasture where the mist still lay in the low spots like fistfuls of quilt stuffing. A path ran obliquely into the pasture and she started out on it, though she didn't know why, since she knew where it ran—to the garbage pit. She'd followed the path out there every day of her life to toss out the trash. It was nothing but a big trench in the ground, maybe thirty feet deep and a hundred long, that her father had hired someone to dig out with a backhoe ten or fifteen years before. It was about two-thirds full of garbage and old junk, and when it was full, Walker would have it covered over and dig another one. She usually paid it no mind at all; she'd just carry the kitchen can out, stand at the edge, and dump it in without so much as looking.

Now she looked. The pit was only a hundred yards or so from the house; she could see the second story and the roof through the trees. The garbage in the pit seemed to be mostly glass jars and milk jugs—they seemed to rise to the top somehow. There were old things down there, too, broken and useless, an old ironing board, part of an old bicycle of Fisher's, a tractor tire Walker had pitched in there a few years back. She felt like she ought to feel sad looking at all the worn and unwanted things her family had collected, but she didn't. Everything has its place in this world, she thought, and there was something serene about the garbage settling down into the rainwater that had collected in the pit.

She walked on past, going around the pile of dirt that had been dug out to make the hole, eroded down now to about half its original size. She went away from the house, out across the pasture, following the narrow tracks the cattle had worn into the dirt. She didn't know where she was going, but it was good to walk. The sand in her shoes gritted with every step, and when she was a few hundred yards from the house she remembered about the canebrake rattlers that liked to lie out on the sand of paths and roads at night and might not have slithered home yet. Normally, she'd wait until the heat of the day had driven them underground to walk out here. She hated the very thought of them. She resolved not to think about them; she resolved to walk wherever and as far as she pleased.

She found herself, after walking the breadth of the pasture to its back boundary, at the old sugar mill. It was brushy around the walls and thick with beggar's lice, and she almost didn't go in. She walked around to the road on the other side and saw where people had been dumping trash, and thought to herself that she'd tell Walker to get the road chained off to keep the trailer trash from driving in with their pickup trucks and tossing whatever they had to throw away and were too lazy to take to the dump onto her father's back pasture. For heaven's sake, there was even a refrigerator lying on its side next to the sugar mill's wall! She felt her lips tighten with distaste. The carelessness of people! The absolute lack of consideration.

Part of the wall next to the road had crumbled since she'd last been to the mill. Or, more likely, some vandal had run into it with his truck and knocked it down. She stepped over the ledge of bricks that was left there and into the weedy middle of the mill. There was a path through the weeds to the hearth and she took it, walking slowly and dragging her feet to give any snakes that might be lying around the chance to hear her and move on.

Most of the chimney, she noted, was still standing, though it didn't look like it would take more than good breeze to take it all down. The hearth was full of brick and something else—she looked closer and it took her a full minute to realize what it was she was looking at. Condoms. A pile of condoms shriveled like snake's skins.

"God in heaven," she said, and started back like just like cow had started from the trough, like she was afraid something was going to bite her. She almost fell, but caught herself. She shuddered, feeling sick to her stomach. She hurried back down the little trail and through the wall and out of the sugar mill. She felt so suddenly exhausted, clear through to her bones, she wondered if she might not be able to make it back to the house. She walked along the road, following the ruts back up to the highway, because it seemed easier. "Oh, God," she said, "O Jesus My Redeemer."

She came to the highway and out from under the trees and the sun was already getting high and hot. She could see little standing waves of heat over the pavement and she walked rapidly along beside the road in the direction of the house. She kept her eyes on the gravel shoulder and tried not to think about the things her mind kept stubbornly wanting to think about. Home, she thought, I'll just go home and have my coffee.

She heard a rushing sound and started to turn and a truck roared by her, carrying a wall of hot air and stinging bits of sand with it. The driver blew his air horn at her and she fell to her knees in the gravel, stunned by the noise and fury of it, and by the sudden stillness of its having passed harmlessly by.

*

When she saw the house again she was sure that even if the Lord himself had asked it of her she couldn't go in. She stood in the dirt of the driveway feeling so restless and upset that she couldn't keep her hands still—they kept touching her hair and side of her face whenever she was not clenching one with the other. Not for the first time in her life she wished she could allow herself the immodesty of pants with pockets, just so she could put her hands into them. Her housedress had no pockets whatsoever, and her hands seemed clumsy with no place to go.

She put her hands into her armpits and walked to the open door of the garage. It wasn't a garage, really. Her father had built it as a machine shed, but it was where Walker kept the car. She looked at the old Buick sitting there and it looked like a quiet and comfortingly isolated place to sit, so she opened the door and sat down. There were little dots of blood on her dress from her knees. She pulled her hem up a little so she could look at them. Both were scraped up and the right one was still bleeding a little from a cut right on the point of her kneecap. She clucked her tongue at herself. She noticed, just above her knee, Walker's keys hanging in the ignition. She looked at them there for a moment, and then, hardly even thinking about it, she started the car. She sat for a minute with it running and thought about turning it off and going inside, but instead she put it into gear and backed out of the garage, then drove down the driveway to the road.

She turned left onto the highway and drove toward town. She had no idea where she was going, but it felt good to be going. She came up on a truck moving slowly up a grade and she mashed the gas pedal to the floor and whipped recklessly around it. When she was even with the truck's cab, she surprised herself by blowing the car's horn. She jerked the wheel and threw the car back into the right lane just ahead of the truck as they crested the rise. There wasn't a car in the oncoming lane, but the idea that there could have been—that a car or a truck or a bus could have popped over the top of the rise and hit her head-on—was wildly intoxicating. She felt her heart beating hard in her chest like it would burst through and land in her lap with a thump and a gurgle. Her face felt numb and her jaw tingled and she wondered if maybe she were just plain going insane, right here behind the wheel of her father's old Buick.

Then she felt suddenly nauseated. There was a church just off the road and she pulled over into its parking lot and her hand went to her face and touched her cheek, the fingers patting the skin beside her nose in a sort of rhythmic tremor. She opened the door and got out of the car. She could feel the heat from the parking lot's tarmac through the thin soles of her house shoes. It was hellishly hot, she thought, as hot as hell, and that was the truth. It was hell, all of it, the whole earth and every-thing in it. The shadows in the church's doorway looked cool, but it was a Catholic church and it felt wrong to even be here standing outside of it, much less to think of going in.

But she went anyway. She felt drawn, beyond herself. She touched the door and then pushed it open and went inside. Unlike most of the churches in town, which were wood-frame, this one was brick and stone and it seemed weighty inside and too cool. The heat outside was cut off by the door shutting and the sweat on her chest and neck seemed abruptly icy cold. There was a stone font half full of very still water beside the inner door. She knew what it was for; she walked on by it. The build-ing seemed deserted, though she knew there must be a priest around.

She walked down the red carpet of the center aisle toward the altar, and every step she took she became angrier. There were idols every-where. She'd been in their churches, had known that Catholics were idolatrous, but she hadn't really felt the depth of it in her heart. A very familiar feeling came over her. She could feel a sort of determination take over the muscles in her body. Her hands ached to hold something, to *wield* something. In her mind's eye she saw St. Michael bearing his wrathful sword. Walker, she thought, you are sure lucky you aren't around.

She strode to the altar and took hold of a big brass candlestick. It was heavy and solid in her hand, an able instrument. She strode to the side of the altar, to the almost life-sized statue of a woman that she guessed was supposed to be the Virgin Mary. Even with its head bowed, the statue managed to look haughty. She swung the candlestick back behind herself for momentum, and brought it down hard across the side of the idol's head. Half of the statue's face cracked and burst in a cloud of dust and sharp-looking fragments of alabaster. She swung again and took off both of the templed hands at the wrist, sending them spinning off under a pew. She hit it two more times, then moved on to what looked to her to be a saint of some sort, its eyes cast piously upwards. She brought the candlestick down square onto his forehead and wiped the piousness clean away.

Then somebody was holding her from behind by her upper arms, shaking her so hard she dropped the dented candlestick on the floor, where it rattled and rolled across the hardwood. "Please!" the priest was saying to her, "for God's sake, please!"

She started to say something back to him, started to tell him what God's sake amounted to in this world, and it wasn't in any catechism, but something took her voice away. The priest held her tight and the first strange thought to cross her mind was how she must look, middle-aged woman in a housedress and mules, her hair unkempt, covered in the chalky dust from broken statues.

And then God descended.

She felt the Holy Spirit take her. Her whole body started to shake and tremor. Strange words filled her mouth, and the tongues poured out. The priest let go of her and she fell to the floor and rolled there, her head jerking and her mouth going a mile a minute, saying things she'd never thought of in a language she'd never heard.

The whole church seemed to fill with rose-colored light. She saw the priest's face loom above her for an instant, a young man with clear eyes

and a strong chin, and then her eyes rolled irresistibly up into her head
and her ears filled with humming. Glory, glory, it filled her from head to
foot. She felt a darkness falling over her like a blanket and first she
thought, *He's taking me home,* and then she thought, *it's about damned time.*

★

Waiting for Fisher, Julia Ross sat on her bed in her room, in her disappointment, and thought about angels—big, righteous, sword-bearing angels, Old Testament and calm, peering down in stolid ranks from on
high. What she had in mind was a heavenly host poised to descend on
the multitudes, to pluck them clean, swift justice on wings of flame.

Angels. She sat with her eyes closed and could see them, and the
sight comforted her mind. When she heard Fisher coming down the hall
she didn't flinch or sway or hold her breath. She smiled, and she was
smiling when he walked through her door, looking tentative and unsure,
and she held out her hand to him and he took it and helped her up from
the bed. His grip was firm, and she thought, What a strong boy!

"We're going, momma," he told her. "Sheriff Park's going to meet us
there."

"Of course," she said, "I know that." She knew she sound waspish,
but that was OK. They couldn't punish her for that. And it just took
more effort than she had in her to try and be nice about everything anymore. Niceness took energy; if people wanted niceness, well, they could
just start looking somewhere else for it. She was through.

Fisher wouldn't meet her eyes. He just said, "Sure," and took her suitcase and headed for the door. He'd never been much for confrontation,
she thought. Never had much spine. That was fine, too. She kept her
head high and her eyes straight ahead until they were out the front door
and she was out of Walker's house and beyond Walker's eyes and his
judgment. Then she let her eyes wander to heaven, the blue sky like
God's own waiting face above, and she stopped dead in the driveway
and fell to her knees and prayed to God her thankfulness.

"Jesus, Mom," Fisher said, but she ignored him. She prayed until she
felt better. She prayed until she felt free to either pray or not, until she
felt something had been satisfied. Then she stood up and brushed the

dirt from her knees. "I'm ready," she told Fisher, and he rolled his eyes and opened the car door.

Fisher kept quiet while he drove. He felt he ought to say something to his mother, but he couldn't quite decide what. It wasn't every day that you drove your own mother to the Chattahoochee State Mental Hospital for evaluation. For twenty minutes or so, he just listened to the car's tires humming on the highway's grooved pavement. He had just decided to try to tell her something about how he felt when she cleared her throat.

"I need to go to the bathroom," she told him.

He thought about that. He thought about saying something about how she should've gone before they'd left the house, but he knew how that would sound, so he just said, "OK," and started looking for an exit with a gas station.

"Any place will do," she said. "It doesn't have to be clean, even."

"All right, Momma, I'll see what can do."

He saw a Texaco sign above the trees ahead, over the first exit into Silver Springs and Ocala, and he pulled off onto the exit and up to the station. He parked beside the gas pumps. "I'll go ahead and get some gas, since we're here," he said. He didn't look at her; he just opened the door and got out of the car and took the pump handle off of its cradle.

"That's fine. I won't be a moment," Julia said. She was slow getting out of the car and he thought about coming around the car and helping her up, but instead he stuck the pump nozzle into the gas tank and started filling it. He kept his eyes on the pump and hardly noticed her making her way between the pumps up to the station. He watched the numbers flicking along on the pump's dials. A breeze kicked up across the concrete between the pumps and threw grit around and blew a piece of blue paper towel between his feet and out onto the road. He just hoped that however things turned out with Julia, it wouldn't make anything harder than it already was. He didn't think he could handle a whole lot more before something inside simply snapped and he took off as quick as he could go for parts unknown. He closed his eyes and tried not to think about it.

Julia pushed open the station's glass door and went inside. The air inside had a spicy smell, like cloves and cinnamon. The girl behind the counter was sixteen or seventeen, heavy and sleepy looking. When Julia asked her for the key to the ladies' room, she peered out the window to where Fisher was filling the car, as if to make sure Julia was actually associated with a paying customer. Then she handed Julia the key, hung on a long piece of plastic with the Texaco star logo printed on it, and the single capital letter "L" in black magic marker. "It's on that side," the girl said, and pointed. "Make sure the door's locked when you leave."

Julia went back out again and around the side of the building. The door to the ladies' room was already ajar. She stood outside the door for a moment, then took the handle and pulled the door closed. She put the key into the lock and left it hanging there, its strip of plastic swinging. Then she turned and walked across the strip of blacktop that ran behind the station and into the field beyond it. The field had been recently bush-hogged, and the walking was rough, stepping through drifts of mown down weeds. The air was full of goldenrod, and she felt the urge to sneeze, but didn't. Her head felt light and full of wool.

Beyond the field was another road going north and south, parallel to the highway. She crossed it and went into the pine woods where a firebreak had been cut through the brush. She followed the firebreak where it ran through the trees down toward a lake. When she got to the lake, she'd follow the shoreline in whichever direction seemed easiest. When she found another road or firebreak or a path leading away, she'd take that. And after that, whatever offered itself. She had the profound feeling that it didn't matter. The Lord would provide direction. Her part was simply to go.

She looked at the light shimmering on the water down below. She took a deep breath, filling her lungs like she was going to dive into it, filled to the brim with sudden glory.

★

It was nearly midnight before Fisher decided to just quit looking. He had driven up and down every two-rut country road, it seemed, that God had ever seen fit to place in the state of Florida. Twice he had stopped at gas stations to use the phone and call his father or the cops, but both times he had decided he just couldn't do it, either one. He could imagine what they'd have to say to him. So he'd just gotten back into the car again and started back looking. Around midnight he found what must have been the only gas station in central Florida still open that late, and found it just as the manager was about to lock the door. He filled the Buick and got a sandwich and a Coke and sat in the car out in the parking lot while the manager turned off all the lights and locked up. He ate the sandwich while he tried to figure out what to do.

This is it, he thought. You've been looking for a reason, and this is it. He had two hundred dollars that Walker had given him in an envelope, meant for the people at the state hospital so Julia could have some things she might want during the two weeks they were going to hold her. He had a car and a tank full of gas. He had north and the whole damned country just waiting.

But he didn't start the car. Except for the stars, there wasn't a light anywhere for as far as he could see through the windshield. It's all too much, he thought. Julia's strength awed him, now that he considered it. The world as open and endless as the broad and scornful face of God, and how to just step out into it? Like a Christian soldier, he supposed, smashing idols and shooting old men for pissing off porches. Walking into the blind distances without a qualm.

The stars burned hot and serious in the night sky, and it suddenly occurred to him what craziness really was. It was knowing. It was certainty. He felt lost and hugely alone.

When he finally started the car and pulled out of the parking lot, it was south he headed instead of north, and he drove fast, both hands hard on the wheel. Cars would pass him going the other way, their headlights so blinding white he had to look away. He watched their taillights in the truck's mirrors, like red stars bulleting crazily away, getting smaller and smaller until, like everything else, they were far and only gone.

A SMALL CHURCH IN
THE COUNTRY

★   ★   ★

After everyone from the Young Adults Group and all of their chaperones have unloaded their bags and bundles from the bus and taken
to their cars and left, after all the good-byes are said and done, Bob
Wenkins drives the bus out of the parking lot. Carol, his wife, walks to
the very back of the bus and sits down sideways, the back of her head
against the window and her eyes, behind sunglasses, turned away from
him.

He drives the half-mile from the church to the house, pulls the bus
into the dirt driveway and parks it, leaving it in gear so it won't roll. It is
very quiet in the bus after he turns the engine off.

"Carol—" he starts.

"Call me Tantra."

"What?"

"Tan," she says, then, "tra."

"Lord, Carol."

"Nothing, don't worry about it," she tells him. She stands up in the
aisle, opens the back emergency door, and jumps down out of the bus. It

is about a four-foot drop and he hears her grunt when she lands and then swear.

"Ah, hell," Pastor Bob says. It sounds loud and blasphemous in the empty bus. He sits in the driver's seat and leans over the steering wheel, his chin on his forearms, and looks through the windshield, speckled with the yellow smears of dead bugs, at their home. A little white frame house near a little country church where a little city pastor preaches. A porch sagging a little on one side; gray shingles on top rimmed with black where the gravel is worn off, curled up like rows of sneering lips. And it isn't even theirs; it belongs to the church members, who let them live here as part of the stipend he is paid for being pastor. We don't even have a *car*, he thinks mournfully, just this big, diesel-stinking bus to get around with, which also, of course, belongs to the church. They *had* a car, a 1972 Ford Pinto which had been old and rusty but at least service-able, but its engine had thrown a cylinder rod less than a week after he had driven it the four hundred miles down from the Columbia Presbyterian Theological Seminary in Atlanta, loaded down with their every worldly possession—which, for a seminary student and his wife, didn't amount to all that much.

Things had never mattered all that much to Bob, though, or at least they'd never seemed to matter much before. They seem to matter more the older he gets. Or maybe it's the more disappointed in himself he becomes. He counsels a number of the members of his congregation about their drinking or their smoking, but he can understand why they never seem able or even willing to give them up. Nobody wants to give up an addiction that makes you feel better than you feel without it. Small indulgences for the weak of will. He had splurged money that they didn't have just a couple of weeks back to buy himself a very nice English briar pipe, though he hadn't smoked since he was an undergraduate and Carol wouldn't let him do it in the house anyway. But it had felt so good to hold that expensive piece of briar in his hand, to own it, to touch match to good Irish flake tobacco and smell that opulent smell. He wants very badly to do that right now; to go back to his little office and hold that warm briar in his palm, round and smooth as a breast.

And, Heaven save him, he wants a car again, so he won't have to cruise around the parking lot at the Piggly Wiggly for a half-hour every time he goes for groceries, trying to find ten spaces in row so he can park the bus.

He wants more and he wants it in an almost helpless way. And Carol. Ah, Lord, he thinks. He leans abruptly back in the driver's seat and puts his hand in his pants pocket and feels for the little, folded-up piece of paper he's been carrying around with him for the last two days. He doesn't take it out. He doesn't want to look at it again. He's read it so many times that he doesn't really need to. He feels the familiar weight of his defeat shiver down inside his belly like a gallon or two of some cold thick liquid, bitter as bile.

They had been together for almost two years when Bob had found his vocation. He and Carol had been going to church together occasionally, maybe a couple of times a month. Carol's family was Presbyterian, but Bob had been bounced around a lot when it came to religions; his mother had moved him and his brother and sister from church to church, and though he'd started out life by being baptized as a Catholic, he'd also been a Methodist and an Episcopalian, and had finally stopped going to church altogether when he was fourteen. But, he realizes, thinking back on it, some germ of faith had been planted in him, and one calm and sunny Sunday morning he had been sitting in the pew with Carol, holding her hand in fact, and he had felt inside himself a great welling of something that was equal parts repentance, awe, and adoration. It didn't seem to have had anything to do with what the minister was saying—as a matter of fact, he couldn't remember what the sermon was about afterward. He thought maybe it was something in the quality of light, a spring morning and the sunlight through the stained glass windows bright and dusty. He'd felt the Lord move inside of him and before he knew it he was weeping right there in the pew, to Carol's considerable consternation.

He'd spent part of the next summer with the Presbyterian Home Missions helping build houses in rural Georgia for people who couldn't afford them. Carol hadn't gone along, but she'd been supportive, and when he came back that summer and told her he wanted to go to seminary, and that he wanted her to marry him, she'd consented. They'd been married the week after graduation from Georgia State, and the week after that, after a honeymoon in Savannah, they'd moved into married-student housing at the Columbia seminary and he'd started the work of becoming a man of God.

He remembers the first few breathless weeks of actually living together. The apartment itself hadn't been much, a two-room arrangement with cinder block walls and a kitchenette to one side of the living room so small that they couldn't both stand in it at the same time in the morning to make coffee and bagels. After he'd been in seminary for a year, she'd gotten a job a school for disturbed children, shepherding kids with mental and emotional problems around the school campus, making sure they got to the classrooms they were supposed to be going to, keeping head counts so she'd know when one had managed to escape so she could call the cops and get him back.

One night he had come home from a late class and found her sitting alone in the dark on the living room couch. He'd sat down with her on the other end of the couch and stayed that way for a while, and when she didn't say anything he asked her, "What's up, sweetheart?"

"Nothing," she said, very strangely, and he'd let it go, thinking it was a mood. She'd been pregnant for almost three months by that time. He figured she'd let him know what was bothering her when she got around to it. And eventually she did, in the small hours after midnight when the breeze blowing through the open windows was finally cool after the long summer afternoon. He'd been listening to the sounds coming through the window with the breeze, a siren wailing off somewhere downtown, a car's horn, a faraway train whistle, all these sad sounds in the darkness, and he had been startled to realize that one of those sounds was his wife moaning to herself, across from him on the other end of the couch.

He had leapt up from the couch and flipped on the lights and there she was, deadly pale, blood everywhere, in her lap and soaked through the couch, and she'd looked down at herself and screamed. He'd scooped her up into his arms and kicked open the front door and ran with her to the Pinto. He'd driven like a maniac, running lights and gunning the Pinto down the deserted, late night streets like sailing through a room. He is sure he never touched the brakes, not even once, the whole way to the hospital.

At the emergency room, someone had whisked her away and he'd sat in the beige waiting area, the panic slowly wearing off, replaced by a ponderous, ineffable sense of dread. In his whole short life, he'd never known a feeling quite like that. He'd never been quite that afraid. He'd gotten down on his knees in that hospital waiting room, knelt down with his elbows on the beige plastic seat of his chair and he'd prayed for mercy, for dispensation. He prayed as hard as he'd ever prayed, some of it out loud, probably. There were more nurses at the desk than he'd remembered. When he'd finally gotten back up off his knees, every one of them was staring at him like he was insane, or at least more than a little strange.

"I'm a minister," he'd said to them by way of explanation, and he'd felt a sharp stab of immediate guilt at even that little evasion. It was no time for sins great or small, he knew, not when one was supplicating the Almighty for miracles. It was sure as hell no time to be worried about appearances. Sit down, he'd told himself, shut up. Trust in the Lord.

The next morning, taking Carol home, he couldn't shake the feeling that he'd known all along, without being able to admit it, that there wasn't going to be any dispensation. He'd had a brief, horrible flash of doubt—or, really, something far beyond doubt, a huge, vacuous sense of loss—that it wasn't a baby that had died, but that God himself somewhere in his deepest Heaven had simply stopped, had been sucked away so there was nothing left of divine grace but the cold, dry snap of the stars in their unspeakable void. He'd shivered and shaken himself like a dog, right there in the driver's seat of that ramshackle old Pinto.

He'd found a way to return to the body of Christ, though. His faith had seeped back into him in calm degrees. Mysterious ways, he'd told himself. You can't second-guess the Lord. He still has that faith, but he seems to be losing everything else in an attrition that picks up its pace day by day—youth, energy, the will toward good that makes an ordinary man a minister to peoples' souls. I'm only thirty-two years old, he thinks bitterly. I shouldn't have to live every day of my life feeling worn through and used up.

"I just don't know how to live my life anymore," he wails aloud in the empty bus. He feels immensely sorry for himself, and guilty for feeling that way. He puts his head down against the hard plastic of the steering wheel and tries to pray, but it won't come. Instead, an image flashes through his head so quickly he can't even begin to try and keep it out: one of the young people of his church kneeling in front of him, looking up at him in supplication with her wide, blue eyes.

"Oh, God," he groans, and beats his head in a gentle, steady rhythm against the steering wheel.

★

Carol doesn't even look up when he comes in from the bus carrying the single suitcase they share because it is the only suitcase they own. She is sitting on the couch with her legs drawn up underneath her. She has a drink in one hand and she is still wearing her sunglasses, though there isn't a light on and it's dim inside the house.

He drops the suitcase in the middle of the floor and says to her, "I can't handle this anymore."

Carol doesn't say anything. She sips her drink. He feels infuriated and ungodly and more than a little sick.

"Do you have any idea how afraid I am for us?"

"Afraid of what?" she says finally.

"Afraid of everything. Afraid that the one thing that really matters in this life is lost on you, and, Lord save us, it's damned near lost on me." He is shaking so hard his knees feel weak, so he collapses down into the dusty armchair across from her. "I'm terrified," he says, "I'm terrified that I've wasted my entire, forsaken life on people who couldn't care less. I'm terrified that I've given away every Heaven-sent thing I have for absolutely nothing. That I haven't changed one thing in this world for the

149

better. I am—" he is gasping now, and has to suck in a ragged breath before he can go on. "I am scared to death that everything I believe, everything I am, might be just *wrong*." He can't believe how self-pitying he sounds, how thoroughly weak and sorry for himself.

She looks at her drink, carefully, like she is studying the glass through the blind distance of her sunglasses. She puts it down on the coffee table. "It must all be pretty humbling, huh?"

He shakes his head irritably. "What?"

"Nothing," she says.

He claws his way up out of the chair and stands leaning over her. She won't look at him. He hovers over her, and he can feel violence threatening in every muscle fiber of his hands and arms. She picks up her drink again and he snatches it out of her hand and flings it against the wall over her head so that it shatters and sprays glass and liquor over them both. "How much of that stuff do you drink, anyway?" he shouts.

She doesn't say anything and he turns away from her and strides across the room, pulling at his hair with both hands. He looks desperately around him for things to throw but there's nothing at hand, so he tears at the buttons of his own shirt and rips it off and wads it and throws it at her. She flinches but doesn't move out of the way and it bounces off of her face, knocking her sunglasses askew. Then he tears off his pants and throws them too, but not at her, just down the hall where they skid in ludicrous loops across the wooden floor.

He stalks over to the couch in his boxer shorts and she cringes back, her eyes wide. He grabs up one of the couch pillows and the vodka bottle hidden behind it. He points at the door with the bottle. "I'm going out to sleep in the bus," he tells her. "I can't stand it inside this house another minute. I will not sleep in here. Not anymore."

He strides to the door and wrenches at it, and when it sticks in its warped frame as it always does in the summer dampness, he moans and kicks at it twice with his bare foot, and then yanks back with his full weight, jerking it free. He strides out and slams the door shut behind him with a violent bang.

Outside, he takes two steps toward the bus and realizes it isn't even dark yet. It's no more than four or five o'clock. He is standing in his front yard in his underwear in the middle of the afternoon, a couch pillow in one hand and a half-empty bottle of vodka in the other. The sky overhead is dark with the promise of rain, and thunder rumbles nearby. "Damn, damn, damn," he says. He grits his teeth together and goes to the bus, pushes the door open, throws the pillow down on the first seat, and throws himself down on top of it.

He twists the top off the vodka bottle, upends it, and takes a drink. It burns his throat, but he takes a second anyway. "Ah," he gasps. Thunder rumbles again overhead and the rain starts, big, fat drops that ping off the bus's roof like tiny, imperious little hammers.

★

Carol sits on the couch alone for a very long time, the room around her getting darker and darker as first the rain comes with all its insistence and soft patter, and then the night, filling all the corners with shadows. She feels like she wants to cry, but it doesn't come. She feels cried out, dried up right through to her core.

After a while she takes a deep, shuddering breath and picks herself up out of the couch. She gathers her husband's shirt and walks down the hall and gets his pants. She opens the hamper in the bathroom and throws in the shirt, and then she goes through the pants pockets and pulls out his keys and his penknife and a folded-up square of paper.

She goes into the bedroom and puts the keys and knife on top of his dresser. She unfolds the paper and reads it.

"Oh," she says. She looks at it for a good, long while, then takes a deep breath, a cleansing breath, as they liked to say in Lamaze classes. So he knows, she thinks. Somebody saw her with the boy, there in the drunken, fumbling darkness, and now he knows. Then she puts the unfolded paper on his dresser beside the penknife and the keys. She can still see the last words on the paper, printed neatly across the bottom. *God knows what's in your heart.*

She goes into the living room, drags the suitcase back into the bedroom, and wrestles it up on top of the bed so she can open and unpack it. She puts the dirty clothes in the hamper and the ones they hadn't gotten around to wearing back in the drawers. She hangs up the two white dress shirts he'd brought along and puts his shoes in the closet on the floor beside a open-topped box full of books.

She looks at the box for a while and turns over one of the books so she can see the cover: *Black Beauty*, it says, *A Weekly Reader's Classic*. It is one of the books from childhood, one that her parents had given back to her when they'd sold the big house in Cartersville, Georgia, where she'd grown up. They'd moved into a condo in Fort Walton Beach.

There were boxes of books in every closet in this house, most of them hers. She'd been an English major. She'd loved the Romantic poets, especially Keats with all his music and melancholy. There weren't any bookshelves in the house when they'd moved in, so Bob had built some with boards and cinder blocks, but they'd only held a couple dozen of her books.

She decides she wants a bath. She takes the book with her when she goes into the bathroom. She puts it on the edge of the pedestal sink and puts the plug in the tub and starts filling it. It is a big, antique-looking tub, claw feet and all. It is raised up on those feet a few inches from the floor, enough so it is hard to get into but not enough so that it is easy to dust under. She pours in some bath salts and strips off her clothes and steps into the hot water and settles slowly in, getting used to it.

After a minute, she sits up and stretches out of the tub to get the book off the sink. She lies back in the water and opens it. On the inside of the cover is her name where she'd written it when she got the book as a twelfth birthday present. She turns to the first page and reads, *The first place that I can well remember was a large pleasant meadow with a pond of clear water in it.* That sounds so pretty that she feels like crying again. She closes the book and puts it down on the floor beside the tub.

When the water starts to cool, she gets out of the tub and walks naked and dripping to the kitchen. In the cabinet where the Tupperware is stored, she finds another bottle of vodka. She takes a coffee cup from the sink and walks back to the bathroom. She sets the cup on the side of the tub and pours it full. Then she runs more hot water into the tub until the water is only a couple of inches from the rim.

She goes to the medicine cabinet and takes down the little amber plastic bottle full of sleeping pills—*Flurazepam*, the label says, mysterious, Latinate-sounding word—and pours them all out into her palm. She counts. There are fifteen of them. She puts two back. Thirteen, for some reason, seems to be right. She puts the bottle back in the cabinet and closes it, then steps into the tub and settles down into the water again.

Very carefully she puts each pill on her tongue and washes it down with a swallow of the vodka, until the pills are gone and the cup is empty. Then she pours the cup full again and takes another swallow, and slides down in the tub until the water is just under her chin.

It feels very comfortable. She feels very calm, though it is too soon, she figures, for the pills and booze to be doing much.

She lies very still and watches the surface of the water spread out like a wriggling plain in front of her. The ripples that bounce around off her head and her knees and the side of the tub become smaller and smaller and finally the water seems almost perfectly still, just the slightest vibration she can barely see, the thin, distant throb of her own heartbeat. The water dimples slightly where the surface tension sticks the skin of the water to the skin of her knees. She looks at that and thinks of reeds in a lake. Cattails, poking up through the water, little water-skaters sliding frantically about, the black jelly-dots of tadpoles wriggling around.

She realizes suddenly she is feeling something after all, a marvelous, smooth sort of lethargy. She feels limp and warm.

This is stupid, she tells herself. Get up. Go over to the toilet and stick your finger down your throat and puke that mess back up.

Hells bells, she thinks. Far too much effort in that.

She shuts her eyes and has a quick little waking dream about being a horse alone in a pasture under a wide, blue sky. It is very peaceful, no one else around for miles and miles, a light breeze blowing the salty-clean smell of the ocean in from somewhere not too far off. After a little while she really does fall asleep, and she doesn't wake even when, a few minutes after that, she slides down the rest of the way in the tub and the warm water closes without a splash over her head.

★

Pastor Bob lets the door slam behind him. He stands just inside the rectory and lets the rainwater stream off of him onto the hardwood floor. The headache he's been nursing all day has moved from between his temples around to the back of his skull, and walking all the way from the house in his underwear in the cold rain hasn't helped. There are aspirin and such in the kitchen attached to the Fellowship Hall, but he doesn't feel like doing anything about the headache. He feels, in fact, like letting it linger.

He goes into his office and sits with a sigh in his desk chair. His boxer shorts and his undershirt stick wetly to him, but it's not so uncomfortable that he feels like doing anything about it. He opens the bottom right drawer and takes out his pipe and tobacco pouch. He fills the pipe and strikes a match but instead of lighting it, he lets the match burn down until the flame scorches his fingertips, and even then he doesn't blow it out; he lets it burn until it runs out of matchstick and puts itself out in the dampness of his own flesh. He sucks at his burned fingers. Then he puts his pipe and pouch back in the drawer and closes it.

Then he opens it again. He takes a brown paper bag from the drawer and sets it on his blotter, then pushes the drawer closed. He leans back in his chair and contemplates the bag for a while, his fingers templed against his face so that the tip of his nose just touches the tips of his ring fingers. Then he sits abruptly up and opens the bag, takes out the object inside, and wads the bag and drops it into his wastepaper basket. He straightens the leather flail out and centers it on the blotter.

The flail is a crude thing. He'd bought it in a pornography shop in downtown Atlanta one evening years ago, when he was restless and couldn't stand to be in his parents' stuffy house any longer. It is basically a short whip, maybe a foot-and-a-half long altogether—a cat-o'-nine tails, though it only has five tails—made of tapering strips of leather stained black and braided together. The handle is wooden and wrapped in the same black leather. He had modified it a little in his father's garage. He had snipped the heads off of a handful of finishing nails with some wire cutters, making angled cuts so that both ends of each nail were sharp. Then he had pierced the fringe end of each tail of the whip with an ice pick and inserted the nails crosswise to so that they made little Xs, the tips pointing out.

He stands up from his desk chair and goes to the window and pulls the blind down. Then he pulls his undershirt off over his head, folds it neatly and places it over the back of his chair. He pushes the chairs off of the oval carpet in front of his desk.

He takes the flail in hand, and holds it so the tails with their finishing nail barbs hang down straight in from of him. He kneels on the carpet, then thinks better of it. He stands back up, picks the carpet up by its edge with his free hand, and flings it into a corner. He kneels down again, hitting his knees hard against the wooden floor. He gives the flail a preparatory shake and the little nails spin.

O full of all subtlety and all mischief! he says, his voice growing louder with each stroke of the whip until he is shouting the words out, *thou child of the devil, thou enemy of all righteousness, wilt thou not cease to pervert the right ways of the Lord?*

★

Life is suffering, he will tell them. That will be the text of Sunday's sermon, and no beating around the bush and couching it in allegory, either. The truth, straight out and clean. Life is hell. Get used to it.

He sits in his desk chair and leans back, carefully, against the towel he's arranged there. He knows he will have to sit motionless for a half-hour or more until the bleeding stops and he can put his undershirt back on. There are a couple of spots high on his shoulder he figures he'll have to bandage. "Christ," he says out loud to no one.

He has opened the window and he can smell the musty smell of the rain and the night outside. It smells sad. It smells, he thinks, like things breaking down and decaying, moldy and old. He imagines men in their houses everywhere smelling that smell and thinking the same thing, a sort of brotherhood of the disappointed. He thinks he can smell the sea, too, not so far away. The smell reminds him of Carol when she's sleeping.

Everything seems so clear. The pain in his shoulders is itself a clarity, spreading all through him. It's like that day when we are children, he thinks, when we all realize exactly who we are. When we realize we are not our parents, or our classmates, or the rules we've been given to live by. We are not anything we thought we might be or hoped we might be. Dreams, hopes, aspirations—even the blinding grace of God. None of it changes the startling fact that you are forever just yourself and nothing else. That's the good news he'll share with his congregation come Sunday morning.

But tonight, he'll go back home, and Carol will be waiting for him. He thinks about the years to come and the oddest feeling of all comes over him. Anticipation. He imagines himself and Carol in a new house somewhere with fresh paint on the walls, carpets, nice linen on the table, the front door cocked open like a dog's ear, the rooms contemplative. It makes his heart ache to think about the almost-contented sadness of it. A kind of breaking-even.

Look what we have, he will tell her. We have here and now. We have God's mercy and the endless possibility of God's grace. God loves us for what we are, and isn't that enough? And what more can we ever ask?

They will lie down beside each other on cool sheets, and as they fall asleep they will be breathing together in easy rhythm. Life isn't hell, he will tell her, it's adjustment. It's knowing that the long days to come will settle out between us, fine as ash. It's the works and days of hands, on and on, forever.

THE GROVE

onny sat in the back of the car with the chickens in the smell and the feathers, making sure that the cage didn't tip over and fluster the chickens. If it did, they might beat themselves bloody against the chicken wire, and they would be harder to sell. His father generally took Donny with him when he went to sell chickens. Raye would run out in the big green Ford Torino to a place he knew near Frostproof. A man there who kept poultry would let him have a couple dozen hens on speculation, and then he'd load them up in a wire cage in the back seat of the car.

Donny despised these trips, though he knew better than to say anything. When they got back into town, Raye would drive slowly through the neighborhoods, first in the poorer part of the white side of town, then in the black neighborhoods south of the citrus-processing plant. He'd sell the chickens for fifty cents apiece. Donny would run up to the doors and knock and tell whoever answered what they had for sale, and if they wanted one, Raye would take one of the chickens out of the cage and grab its head in one hand and fling it up and around, snapping his wrist like he was trying to crack a bullwhip so that its neck would break.

Then he'd hold the quivering chicken and cut off its head and feet with an old butcher's knife and take his four bits and they'd drive on.

Most everyone knew Raye. Some days, Donny hardly had to get out of the car. The kids in the street would see the green Torino coming and would run in to tell their mommas. Women seemed to like Raye's chickens, killed by hand and fresh so they didn't taste like a supermarket cooler. They'd make ten dollars or so and Raye would get tired of killing chickens and just open the cage and sweep the last two or three out into the street where they'd wander around until somebody caught them for supper or a passing car hit them.

Then Raye would drive to the ABC liquor store. Donny would wait in the car with the windows rolled down so he wouldn't strangle from the smell of chicken dung, and Raye would go in and buy a bottle of Bacardi or RonRico, if he felt especially flush, or a bottle of the store brand rum. He didn't care for the store brand much; it was made from citrus sugar instead of cane, and so it made his head ache. Sometimes he'd be inside for a couple of hours, because the liquor store fronted on a narrow little bar with a half-dozen stools in it, and if he had extra money, he would feel obliged to spend most of it there.

Sometimes he'd come out quick after getting the bottle and they'd drive over to the pool hall where Raye would shoot eight ball. He'd buy Donny a Coke and bag of chips and Donny would sit against the wall and watch him shoot. Raye had his own cue in a slick, black leather case that he kept in the trunk of the car so Donny's mother wouldn't know about it, and Donny was proud, watching him play. Everybody liked Raye.

Donny's mother worked as a waitress at a Mexican restaurant on the highway, but the money was awfully thin around the house. They had no phone, and more than once the power had been turned off. Once he had come home from school to find his mother pleading with a workman from the local utility company who had come to take the meter from the pole outside the back door. The fellow had taken the meter anyway. His mother had cried like her heart would break and Donny had stood there holding his books and feeling dumb because he didn't know anything to say to make it better.

His mother worked the evening shift and left pretty much as the school bus with Donny on it pulled up. If she had time she'd give him something to eat before she left, and then he was Raye's responsibility for the rest of the day. Once she had taken him into the kitchen while Raye was back in the bedroom and had knelt down on one knee beside him. She wore a red-checkered waitress's uniform with broad, white, spotted lapels that smelled like burned grease no matter how much she washed it. She had whispered to him. She had told him, "Your brothers are old enough, but not you." She had told him, "Wherever Raye goes you just stay with him. That's what matters. Don't let him forget and leave you somewhere." So Donny pretty much kept Raye in sight except when he was in the bar, and even then he figured he was fulfilling the spirit of his mother's wishes because he was in the car and Raye wouldn't leave without the car.

Raye didn't seem to mind him though, because Donny was mostly quiet and just went along. Donny was a watcher. That's how he thought of himself. He watched people. He looked at things. It was comfortable and easy and distant and everybody liked him for it, though in a different way than the way they liked Raye. They liked Donny because though he was nine years old he paid attention and kept his mouth shut. Donny could pay attention like nobody's business.

He spent a lot of time watching his mother and Raye. Raye was nice enough to his mother though she complained about him not doing much. That was a lot more than you could say about a lot of men, she had told Donny. Raye told jokes and made his mother laugh and she seemed glad to have him around. I couldn't live without your daddy, she told Donny. Donny paid attention when Raye told jokes. He listened close and memorized them and saved them up like gold and jewels, a horde he could use someday so that someone couldn't live without him, either.

★

Raye drove to the ABC liquor lounge and went in, and when he came back out an hour later he had a bottle of rum and a woman with him. She was blond and pretty and seemed young even to Donny, slim and very serious-looking, drinking RonRico and Coke from a soda can as they drove out to a grove off of the highway east of town. She poured some into an empty can for Donny, and Raye didn't say anything.

"Here, honey," she told him, "this'll make you feel good."

"Thank you," he said and took the can, and she smiled at him and turned back to Raye.

There were already two cars parked beside the irrigation pond when they arrived, four or five men and another woman drinking and talking, a fire going. Donny sat in the car and listened to the party. There were parties at the house, too, sometimes, when his mother was home. Raye never brought people into the house when she wasn't home. It was something they had agreed on. Donny liked the parties, though afterwards the house smelled of cigarette smoke for days and his mother and Raye felt bad and sometimes his mother threw up and sometimes she cried. But the parties were loud and happy and everybody seemed to have a good time. The women who came to those parties were always especially nice to him. They called him "baby," and gave him things, like key rings or candy out of their purses. One woman who was very drunk at the time had gone out to her car and brought back a kaleidoscope for him, a little tube the length of his hand carved out of dark wood and filled with bright bits of glass. He had keep it hidden in the toe of an old tennis shoe he had outgrown but his mother had thrown the shoe out one day while he was at school and the trashmen had gotten it.

He heard a shout and somebody threw a bottle into the orange trees so that it crashed through the branches. He peered out the window to see the blond woman stoop and pick up Raye's half-full bottle of rum and step up to a man and very deliberately swing it up in a smooth arc like pitching a baseball underhanded so that it cracked hard against his left temple. Donny expected the bottle to burst, but it didn't. The man dropped to his knees, and knelt there blinking for a long moment before slouching with a groan over onto his face.

"You don't talk like that to me," she shrieked at him. He lay face down in the sand and didn't answer her. Everyone seemed to be too surprised to move. Then she kicked him in the ear with the sharp toe of her shoe, and a couple of the men started to move toward her. She still held the rum bottle in one hand, swinging slightly back and forth, and stared them down. A third man walked around behind her and grabbed her, locking his arms together under her breasts and pinning her arms to her sides. Raye stood up from where he'd been sitting by the fire but he didn't say anything yet and Donny felt a sudden, sharp anxiety that Raye might not do anything at all, that he might let them hurt her.

The man who held her lifted her up off the ground and squeezed and she bowed her head down like a snake and bit him hard on the forearm. "You bitch!" he yelled. He was a big man, probably twice as heavy as she was, and he squeezed hard and Donny heard her gasp and saw her eyes go wide. Donny could see blood in a small crescent on the man's forearm.

Raye was a relatively small man, under six feet and slight. But as he'd told Donny time and again, he'd grown up hard, with a father who beat him and made him fight, a tomato farmer who was bitter in his poverty and his hardships and made his children suffer for it. The woman was struggling hard, her mouth gaping open for breath. Raye stepped up quickly behind the man who was holding her and jabbed him hard, twice, in the right kidney. The fellow dropped the woman and groped for his back and as he turned Raye hit him twice again, just under his jaw. He stumbled away down to the edge of the irrigation pond. "You chickenshit motherfucker," he yelled. His voice sounded mushy, as if he were having to chew the words to get them out. "I'll kill you. By God, I'll rip your fucking head off." He leaned out over the water and hawked and spit, then stood up straight and started for Raye.

Raye didn't wait. He started away from the cars to meet him. Somebody hissed at him as he passed and Donny caught the word "knife." Then they met and Donny couldn't see anything except a rolling, struggling mass like a quavering shadow bucking across the sand by the pond. Then Raye was loose somehow and the big man was staggering and falling back, and more quickly than Donny could follow in the dim light it was over and Raye had shoved the other man into the pond. Raye slowly walked back up to the car, and the big man stood alone, stooped over in the knee-deep water, and Donny could hear him coughing and weeping.

Raye walked straight up to the Torino without a word. Just as he put a hand on the car door, somebody stepped up and hit him hard across the back of his head with a beer bottle. Donny snatched at the door handle and yanked the door open so he could get out and save him.

Someone was standing over Raye, kicking him in the stomach. Donny bolted out of the Torino and hit the man running with all of his seventy-five pounds. The fellow lurched and then turned and picked up Donny like he was a bushel sack of grass seed and pitched him at the car. Donny slammed into the Torino's rear quarter panel with his shoulders, his head bouncing off the green sheet metal. It knocked him breathless, and for a long minute he couldn't make his eyes focus. He lay there in the sand, feeling the sandspurs pricking through his shirt. He heard somebody yell and a car start. Another car started and there were the sounds of engines roaring and wheels spinning in the dry brown sand. He didn't look up. He was scared to move. For the first time in his life he didn't want to see anything. He wanted to be small, even smaller than he already was. He wanted to disappear. He wanted everything else, everything that wasn't him, to disappear. He almost felt he could make it happen. He felt like he could become a simple black button against an empty field of white, like a dot of ink on a sheet of clean paper. All he had to do was keep his eyes closed.

He opened his eyes. All of the other cars were gone. He saw Raye lying still in the sand near the Torino's front tire. He made himself stop crying and sit up.

He could smell something burning in the fire, plastic or rubber, and a wave of nausea sent a sour mouthful of rum and Coke back up his throat. The jap grass rustled in the darkness underneath the trees and the blond woman walked out into the dying firelight. Donny watched her warily walk up to Raye and kneel down beside him. Raye still didn't move.

Donny climbed into the car so that he was sitting behind the steering wheel. The woman came to stand by the driver's side door, her shoulders hunched and her arms crossed over her chest. Donny looked at her and didn't know what to say to her. She leaned in close to him, like she had something important to say. Like she was going to tell him a secret that meant everything. She smelled of rum and the waxy odor of lipstick. She touched his face. "Oh, honey, I'm sorry," she said.

Donny peered into the shadows that hid her eyes from the moon's thin light, his cheek warm from her touch. He thought of Raye, lying in the sand. He thought of Raye with this woman, this girl smelling of rum and perfume and leaning so close he could feel her body the way the blind can feel walls without touching them, the substance of it like the soft weight of water. He could feel something new pearl up inside him, a sad longing, strange as desire, squeezed small and hard as the green oranges hanging all around like dead birds in the darkness.

She kissed him on the forehead. "I got to go. I can't have this kind of trouble."

She shoved the door closed and Donny watched her walk through the moon- and firelight between the trees until she dropped out of sight into the darkness. He waited what seemed like a long time, and then he opened the door. Raye was a shadow on the ground, hunched and quiet. Donny started walking in the direction the girl had gone, the sand pulling at his feet like sorrow. Then he began to run, faster and faster, until he was running as hard as he could, following her, whoever she was, wherever anyone might lead him for the rest of his life.

GHOST RIVER

★　　★　　★

The first day of the Young Adults Group campout, lunch was hot-dogs cooked on a propane grill and did not, to Fisher's considerable disappointment, involve any elbow rubbing with girls whatsoever. Separate tables for the ladies, a watchful parent at the end of each table. The rest of the day was camping stuff, canoeing on the river and swim-ming—the girls in actual swimsuits, and actually swimming with the boys, though no boy would have dared come closer to one than spitting distance, Fisher imagined. The parents already looked as if the amount of exposed skin was awfully close to too much. There was a good deal of walking up and down the paths that meandered alongside the river, looking for nothing much but looking anyway, under the upturned roots of trees that had been undercut by the river, into gopher turtle burrows, through rafts of water hyacinths and thick stands of fireflag, between the knobby roots and knees of the cypress trees where they poked up out of the river and ridged like fingers through the moss on the banks.

Fisher found a small water moccasin lying on the wrong, dry side of the path and teased it into striking at a stick while a couple of the girls and an elder looked on. The parent, a thin, scholarly-looking woman who wore chino slacks and a pair of tortoise-shell glasses hung from a cord around her neck, looked suitably impressed. The girls tried to look indifferent, but everyone watched without a word until the snake managed to get past Fisher and his stick and slither without a splash into the safety of the water.

"What did that poor snake ever do to you?" one of the girls— her name was Donna Robins—asked, after the snake had swum off.

Later, remembering that question, he would be amazed that he ever allowed himself to trust her. At dinner, as everyone waited in line for chicken cooked on the propane grill, Donna Robins slipped him a note folded so many times that it made a neat, fat, little triangle no larger than a quarter when she pressed it into his palm. He looked at the note and looked at her, but she had already turned her back to him and begun to talk to the woman dishing up the chicken.

Meet me at midnight by the river, it said. "No," Fisher said out loud, not meaning that he wouldn't do it but rather that he couldn't believe it. The woman handing out the chicken thought he meant *no* to the drumstick she was delivering to his plate, and she put it back on the grill and gave him a wing instead.

The rest of the evening was achingly slow. More prayer, of course, and some tedious talk about what Pastor Bob described as "The Meaning of Devotion in the Modern Context." Then the bonfire was lit and Pastor Bob broke out his guitar and everyone sat around the fire and sang along self-consciously. Fisher spotted Donna, and then sat among the rest of boys he shared a cabin with, as far from her as he could manage.

He looked around at his cabinmates, good boys all of them, clean-cut and sincere. One of them, a tall, dark-haired boy about Fisher's age named Wallace Jenkins was planning to go to seminary to become a minister. Fisher felt both disdain and a little envy for him. Conviction virtually snapped in Wallace's eyes; he was all eagerness, sitting with his shoulders hunched forward, watching the bonfire as if it were at once the purifying fire of grace and the flaming gateway to perdition and he could hardly keep himself from leaping in. Fisher had to resist an urge to give him a push and help him get on with it.

Roasted marshmallows, more songs, one last prayer from Pastor Bob and the first day of the Young Adults retreat was over. Everyone broke up and headed for the cabins, and after a flurry of toothbrushing and little prayers whispered beside army cots, the retreat went to bed, young adults and all. It was barely ten o'clock. Fisher lay in his cot under a sheet, the scratchy army blanket wadded over his feet. There were a few stirrings, cots creaking as people adjusted themselves for sleep, and then nothing but the low-grade grinding of the cicadas counterpointed against the tree frog's constant, high-pitched peeping. Fisher lay very still and waited, checking the glowing numbers on his Timex every few minutes.

Around eleven-thirty he found he just couldn't wait anymore. He sat up very slowly on his cot to keep it from creaking and slipped his feet into his shoes. He stood up and edged a few inches at a time toward the door, listening and watching the lumpy scattering of shadows in the cots, freezing once when someone said suddenly in his sleep, "Well, change it then."

There was a yellow floodlamp mounted on a pole next to the bridge over the creek that separated the girls' cabins from the boys'. Fisher stayed in the shadows, and made his way down to the river's edge. He listened to the river for a while, a quiet drip and trickle punctuated occasionally by a splash as a fish rolled or a muskrat or snake flopped off a log into the water. Then he sat down and took off his shoes and rolled his pants legs up above his knees. He was going to have to wade through the mouth of the creek where it fed into the river; there was no using the bridge, out there in the open, in the light, where any of the chaperones, restless and unable to sleep as chaperones tended to be, might catch him.

The moon was full and high over the river and it was easy enough to see where he was going. He walked the narrow path along the bank until it came to the creek, and then he waded out into it, the cold water coming up to the middle of his calves, the mud squishing up between his toes. On the far side he dried his feet on the moss and put his shoes back on. When he stood up he saw her, sitting on the bank a dozen yards away, silhouetted against the moonlight dogging across the river.

He came up quietly and she didn't see him until he was very close. She was sitting on the bank looking out across the water at something he couldn't see, her knees tucked up under her chin. Then something, some sound he made or a change in the quality of air, told her she wasn't alone and she started and turned and he saw the moonlight flash off the lenses of her glasses and he knew with a sudden and terrible certainty that it wasn't Donna.

"Who are you?" Pastor Bob's wife wanted to know.

"Ah—" Fisher said. He was wondering if she'd recognize him later if he simply turned right now and ran back through the creek and up the road as far and as fast as he could run. He couldn't make himself turn, though. She was looking right at him and her gaze held him there, helpless. He waited for her to start yelling and bringing the camp down around them, thirty pairs of accusatory eyes and Donna telling everybody, "A sneaking pervert. I told you so."

Instead, Pastor Bob's wife turned back to look at the river. "Well, if you won't tell me who you are, you can just go away, then," she said. "Go on. Shoo."

"Fisher Ross," Fisher said.

"Oh. The new kid in town."

"Yeah, I guess so. Sort of. I just started with the Young Adult Group."

"I know. I keep the list. It's one of my grand responsibilities as church wife. So what brings you down here? The scenery? The moonlight? High hopes?"

"I don't know," Fisher said, feeling very dull.

"Oh. Well, that's about what I would expect, I guess."

"I think I better get back to the cabin."

She looked up at him again, the moonlight on her glasses flat planes of pale light. "Do you ever look at the stars, Fisher Ross?"

"Sure," Fisher said, though he really didn't make much of a practice of it anymore.

"Sit down," Pastor Bob's wife told him, "I want to show you something."

Fisher thought about it. He figured he could still take off and nothing much would come of it. Hell, he could just hit the road, for that matter. He could get home easy enough, find a phone, call his old man if he had to. He was only here in the first place because his mother had wanted it, and he didn't even know where she was anymore.

"Go ahead, sit down," she insisted. "I don't bite."

"I think I'd rather stand," Fisher said.

She shrugged, a small gesture with just one shoulder. "Whatever. Suit yourself. Look out there," she said, and pointed out toward the sky over the river, the moon full and soft as a blister above the trees, sheared in half by a thin feather ruff of black cloud. "You see that bright little star right above the moon? That's Mars. God of War. Universal symbol for all that is testosterone poisoned. That is the life principal in all its glory, little bitty yin, great big yang, big, dull, womb-shaped yang thing and little pinprick yin thing hovering right on top of it. Pinprick oppression."

"What?"

"Mars, pinprick. Moon, womb. Just *look*, you dipstick."

Jesus, he thought, she's drunk as a skunk. "I don't understand," he told her, and thought about bolting off through the creek and back to the male side of the camp where he belonged.

She leaned over and grabbed suddenly at his rolled up pants leg and hauled him close. "Sit!" she commanded. He sat. She put her hands on his cheeks and pointed his face out above the river so that he was look-ing at the moon where it hung in the sky over the trees. "Moon," she said. "Womb. Yes?"

"Yes."

She shifted his head up a few degrees. "Mars. Pinprick. Yes?"

"OK."

"Where is it?" she said.

"In space."

"No, dummy. Where is it in relationship to the *moon?*"

"On top."

"*Yes*," she said triumphantly. "Bingo. You figured it out. It's on top. Male force doing what male force does. But it's only on top for *now*. Things change, you know."

"Sure," he said. "I guess so."

"You're goddamn right," she said, and then put her hand over her mouth. "Have to watch that. Loose lips."

"Mrs. Wenkins—"

Here," she said, "have a drink."

She handed him the bottle from between her feet. She watched him take a sip and then took the bottle back. "Well, you're not the good boy you're pretending to be, anyway," she said.

"I don't guess so."

"That's fine. I won't tell." She leaned in close to him and he could smell the rum again, wistful and heady on her breath. "And I really don't give a shit if you tell on me."

"OK."

"That's good. Good common ground, is that." She lay back, looking up into the sky. She seemed to be finished talking.

Fisher started to rise. "Well—" he said.

"Look," she interrupted. She pointed up and out above her head. Fisher turned and looked up into the sky again. "Orion. The three stars all in a row there are his belt. The middle one is called Alnilam, or so I was told in my astronomy class back at old Georgia State. I don't re-member the other two. The four stars there, there, there, there," she said, jabbing a finger at each one, "are his shoulders and his knees. Those stars, descending from around the belt area, around old Alnilam there, aren't what you might think they are. They are only his sword, I'm afraid, forever in its sheath. Orion is a pinprick, too."

She turned her head to look at Fisher, her arm sinking down so that her hand came to rest palm-flat on her chest. The moonlight flashed again from her glasses. "Are you a pinprick, Fisher Ross?"

"I don't know."

"You don't know. Why don't you know?"

"Look Mrs. Wenkins—"

"Call me Tantra. Out of respect for the moon."

"Look," he said again, and she reached over and grabbed him by his shirt collar and pulled him down close.

"Look yourself," she said. She let go of his collar and started undoing the buttons on her blouse. She pulled open her blouse and let her hands drop away to her sides. Her breasts were very small in the dim moonlight, convex rises topped with the dark spots of her nipples. When he didn't do anything, she took one of his hands and placed it on one of her breasts. He could feel her nipple, like a gumdrop under his palm. Startled, he took his hand away and stood up and she started crying. She put her hands over her face and rolled over so her back was to him, her knees drawn up to her stomach. The bottle of rum fell over and he could hear the rum chugging its way out, the sound a strange sort of complement to the slower and more subtle gurgling of the river.

"I'm sorry," he said.

"Pinprick," she said, and began to cry harder.

"Oh, shit," Fisher whispered. He stood up. He walked backward a few steps, looking at Pastor Bob's wife crying on the riverbank, and then he turned around and splashed his way into the creek. He stopped halfway across and looked back. Pastor Bob's wife was still there, still lying with her back to him, though he couldn't tell whether or not she was crying any more. For an instant he was sorely tempted to go to her. But he bit his lip and kept going through the creek's mouth back to the male side of the camp, the yin side, and went back alone to his cabin.

*

"It's white!" was the first thing Donna Robins heard when she woke, and in her sleep-fogged mind she thought they meant an angel, because that's what she'd been dreaming about, a great angel, white as a bedsheet, hovering over her head and whispering things in her ear she could almost but not quite understand. But she knew, in the dream, what the angel wanted from her—it wanted her to hurry, to run, to move as fast as she knew how, and the angel, a sweet, sad looking woman with long hair that looked golden one moment and then bright silver the next, had looked so hopeful for her that she'd wanted to cry and she'd run and run and then someone had yelled It's white and she'd woken.

Donna sat up in her cot and rubbed her eyes and saw that it was still

170

nearly dark, the light in the windows pearl gray and dull. One of the other girls, a short, fat seventh-grader named Tina Tierney, was standing in the door and she yelled again, "It's white! Wake up, come look at the river!" Then she turned around and dashed back outside.

"What's with her?" someone muttered sleepily.

"Leave me alone," someone else moaned.

"What's white?" Donna said, thinking of the angel but realizing she had only been part of a very strange dream. No one seemed inclined to answer, so she dressed and slipped her feet into her tennis shoes and went outside to find out for herself. Everything was damp and misty outside, a pale fog hovering over the river. Tina was kneeling by the bank looking at the water. Maybe she means the mist, Donna thought. She walked up behind her and asked again, "What's white?"

"The water," Tina said. She sounded awed and a little afraid. "It's all white."

It *was* white. Donna knelt down beside Tina and put her hand into it. The river was sheet-pale, angel-pale, opalescent, a blueness to it like skin. "It's a dream," she said, and she thought, *I must still be asleep.* But the water was cold on her hand and across the river, lost somewhere in the mist, a mockingbird trilled, and in dreams, she knew, there aren't those sorts of details, like mockingbird songs and the slick feeling of water on your fingers, only the great, gross intimacy of meaning, everything mutable and indistinct. This was real, sure enough.

"What do you think it is?" Tina asked. "Do you think God did it?" Donna was thinking about the story of Jesus turning water into wine. She was thinking about the practical joke she'd pulled on Fisher Ross and the pastor's wife, and she was afraid that the white water was meant for her, an omen or a missive, God's caveat to her that she'd better watch her step. She felt humbled and contrite.

"I'm sorry," she said aloud, but she said it in a very small voice and even Tina didn't seem to notice. She was too busy letting the ghostly water run through her fingers as if she weren't afraid of it at all.

★

Later in the morning, Pastor Bob talked to a service station attendant who'd heard the news on the radio. Sometime during the night, the river had undercut the dike on a holding pond at an open-pit phosphate mine ten miles up the river and spilled close to a billion gallons of phosphate-and-chemical-laden wastewater into itself.

Pastor Bob stood on the riverbank with the Young Adults and the elders and everyone watched the chalky river water flow by, the fireflag and the water hyacinths already looking, everyone agreed, a little sickly.

"Well," Pastor Bob said, "I'm sorry to say it, but I guess maybe we ought to cut the retreat a little short and head on home."

"What about the *dance?*" one of the girls complained.

Pastor Bob bit his lip and considered. He looked at a couple of the adults, who shrugged. "Well, I don't suppose one more night out here will kill us. They didn't say it was actually *dangerous* or anything." He grinned a little bit at them, made a little joke of it. "Just don't anybody go swimming, OK?"

"Swimming," Fisher muttered, "Jeez." He didn't think he'd said it loud enough for anyone to hear, but Pastor Bob turned and gave Fisher a glance that chilled him through. Fisher clamped his mouth shut and looked at his feet.

Pastor Bob's wife made it to lunch, and though she was wearing a pair of dark sunglasses, she seemed otherwise no worse the wear for the rum. So far as he could tell, she never gave Fisher so much as a glance. He ate his hamburger, sneaking glances at her once in a while where she sat with Pastor Bob, her elbows on the table as she ate, her thin arms over her still thinner chest. When he was finished, he went back to the cabin to wait out the rest of the afternoon.

Donna went back to her cabin, too, after lunch. It was the first chance she'd had to do so; her morning had been filled with activities considerably more ambitious than the horseshoes game the men had come up with. One of the mothers had brought crochet hooks and a paper grocery sack full of yarn, and she had corralled a number of the girls in the gazebo and had gotten them to crochet little square potholders. Donna had made a green one for her mother, though it was a little lopsided because she hadn't paid as much attention to making the thing as she probably should have. It was mindless work, and Donna didn't have much patience for mindlessness.

So Donna didn't make it back to the cabin until after lunch, and it was only then, when she was straightening up her bedclothes the way her mother had made her do every day since she could remember, that she found the note, folded into a neat, tight triangle, lying on top of her blanket.

She opened it. *I saw Fisher Ross with Carol Wenkins beside the river last night*, it said. And then, at the bottom, it said, *God knows what's in your heart*. She held her breath. The note seemed like a bolt out of heaven, arbitrary and devastating.

It wasn't signed. Donna folded the paper up again and slipped it under her pillow.

She sat down on the cot to think. A strange, lambent sort of light breathed in and out of the single room of the cabin, cut into long strips by the fronds on the cabbage palm right outside the near window. No one else had come back yet from lunch; they were all down at the river again, watching the milky water flow by.

Fisher Ross, she thought. Why should I care? she asked herself. I don't, she thought, not about Fisher Ross, even if he had done it with the Pastor's wife, which she didn't believe.

She made up her mind, and the rest of the afternoon was colored gray with her resolve. She sat quietly by herself while the other girls played volleyball or sat whispering about boys in little groups under the trees or on top of the picnic tables. She didn't talk to anyone over the supper of barbecued brisket and potato salad. After supper, she went with the other girls to dress for the dance, and there on her cot was her pillow, but not where she'd left it, and the note was gone. Her face felt hot.

She sat on the cot while the other girls dressed, her hands between her knees. Tina, brushing her hair, came over and sat down beside Donna.

Aren't you going? Tina asked. She leaned her head to the side, pulling the brush through her hair.

Donna shrugged, a little gesture, with just one shoulder. "I don't know. I guess so."

"Oh, OK, cool," Tina said, and stood up and walked away. Donna waited until everyone else had left the cabin, and then she put on her hose and the yellow cotton dress that her mother had said made her eyes look so pretty.

At the dance, Donna strode right past the other girls to where Fisher stood under the bare bulbs that lighted the gazebo, and she took his hand and led him out onto the dance floor, though the music hadn't started yet and there was nothing to dance to.

So she stood there in the middle of the empty floor with Fisher, who held her hand and stared at her, until she felt how everyone's eyes were on her and the color rose in a hot flush up her neck and across her cheeks. Everyone had stopped talking and the reedy grinding of the cicadas, who had tuned up into a generous roar as the sun had gone down, seemed suddenly overwhelmingly loud.

"What's the matter, dear?" one of the mothers said brightly. She was sitting in a folding chair on the gazebo's periphery, ready to play the part of preceptor, to step in and explain why a certain necessary distance must be maintained between dancers.

"I'm coming apart," Donna told her without actually looking at her. "Just to pieces, that's all."

"I don't understand you, dear." The mother smiled and tried to look supportive.

"Oh, hush," Donna told her, and walked off the floor and out into the growing shadows beyond the gazebo's light. The mother called out "Dear?" one more time and Fisher imagined he could hear the buzz of gossip starting up among the gathered membership of the Young Adults Group, a sound even more pervasive and shrill in his imagination than the din the cicadas made. He waited a few minutes to give everyone a chance to start thinking of something else, and then he followed her. She hadn't gone far, just underneath the trees at the edge of the clearing. When he came up to her she held out her hand and he took it.

"Come on," she said. She led him out of the camp and up the river path. They walked for what seemed to Fisher a very long way. The moon had started to rise, and though it was nearly full, long streaks of clouds cut out a good deal of its light, so he had to trust Donna to keep them on course, wherever it was they were going.

Where they were going, it turned out, was a beach of sorts, a bend in the river where the slowing water on the outside curve had piled up a bar of sandy silt six or seven yards wide. Donna let go of his hand and went out on the bar to the water's edge. She lifted her arms like she was going to proclaim something to the river, then she seemed to think better of it and hugged them around herself as if she were suddenly cold.

"Oh, hell," she said.

"What is it?"

She turned to look at him. "You don't know anything, do you?"

"What do you mean?"

He couldn't see her face but he could see her shake her head in what he took to be disgust. Somewhere on the path, one-handed, she had let her hair down and it was long and dark and moved like a shadow in the lapsing moonlight that filtered down through the clouds.

"I mean nobody knows anything, do they?" Her voice was tight and he could hear the tears in it, ready to burst out. He felt awkward and confused. He wanted to go take her in his arms and hold her and tell her he'd take care of it, whatever it was, but he was afraid. So he didn't do anything at all.

"And you know less than just about anybody, don't you, Fisher Ross?"

"I know a few things," he told her.

"Yeah, I believe that." Her voice said that she didn't believe it at all. She took her shoes off and then, amazingly, lifted her dress up above her hips and started tugging at the waistband of what Fisher assumed was her panties. "Pantyhose," she corrected him without his having even asked. She quoted, "A Christian lady always wears hose with a dress." She stripped the hose down quickly and the dress fell back into place with only the faintest flicker of white panties in the dim moonlight. She tossed the wadded pantyhose onto the sand and waded a little way into the river, the water around her calves throwing back ripples of light.

"Come on in," she said.

"Jesus, Donna. There's chemicals and shit in that water. It could be toxic."

"Maybe. Maybe not," she said. "I guess you could just wait and see if I die."

"It might take a while, for you to actually die," he told her, just a little sarcastically. "I'd guess it'd have to soak up through your feet for quite a while. And then you probably wouldn't die. Stuff might rot off, toes and the like—"

"Oh, that's nice."

Fisher shrugged, though he wasn't sure if she could see it. "They're your feet."

"My feet," she said. Then, abruptly, she sat down in the water, making a flat splash that sounded loud in the darkness. "My butt, too, I guess," she said, and then, "Jesus, the water's cold."

Fisher pulled off his shoes and socks and started to roll up his pants legs, and then he saw that Donna was pulling her wet dress off above her head and he stopped.

"Can't swim in a dress," Donna said. She threw it up onto the sand and it landed with a damp flop. Fisher felt that sound in his gut, like a quick jolt of electricity just below his belly button. Her white bra and panties were stark, almost fluorescent, Fisher thought, against her only slightly darker skin. She waded out and dove into the water.

Well hell, Fisher thought. He considered for a moment and then undid his belt and his fly and shucked his pants off, and then his shirt, pulling it off over his head without fooling with the buttons. He laid them down high on the sand near the bank and then walked out in his underwear into the water where Donna waited, head and shoulders above the rippling surface.

"It's not very deep," she said, "but it sure is cold."

"And toxic," Fisher said. "Don't forget toxic."

"Who cares?" she said.

"Me either," Fisher told her. He waded out, the water rising over his knees and up his thighs. He expected it to feel viscous or gritty, but it just felt like water, cold and slick. He leaned into the water and pushed smoothly out across it.

Donna stood her ground as he glided up. He stood upright in front of her, head and shoulders out of the water, the current tickling its way around him and trying to tug his feet out from underneath. He could feel the bottom weeds brushing eerily around his ankles. They just stood that way for a while, not touching, the river flowing between them.

"What now?" Donna whispered.

"I don't know," Fisher said, but his hands seemed to move of their own volition up from his sides, through the moving water, up her goosebumped belly and under the tight elastic of her bra, pulling it up over her breasts. Then his hands moved around her, drawing her through the water into his arms so her bare chest pressed against his own.

"Oh," Donna said, and, "oh." The muscles in her legs seemed suddenly weak. Oh, Lord, she thought, I should stop this, but she knew she wouldn't. When he kissed her, she kissed him back, hard, and felt his teeth click against her own. This is crazy-stupid, she thought, but she held him, and felt, she thought, his heartbeat, a distant pulse made insistent by the slick film of water squeezed between their skins.

He helped her back up the sandy slope of river bottom and she spread her wet dress out on the sand and lay back on it. He knelt down to lay beside her and started kissing her again and his kisses moved down her chin to her neck and she felt him tug at her panties and she knew she was lost, that there was no going back, and she didn't care, not even a bit, and she held his head while he kissed her and then his weight pressed into her and left her suddenly breathless. There was no place to tell him to stop, no will to tell him anything.

She held him and kissed his face as he moved against her and then he moaned and just like that, it was over. In the darkness, with the moon in the trees and Fisher's breath soft against her neck, she shivered.

She pulled away from him and tried to sit up and felt suddenly dizzy. "What?" he asked.

"Everything smells green," she said. Everything did. It wasn't an especially good or bad smell. It was just everywhere.

"I guess so," he said.

She found her bra and put it back on and peered around into the dimness looking for her panties. Fisher found them first and handed them to her and she felt a sudden and terrifically intense flush of embarrassment. She stood and slipped them on quickly. He picked up her dress and snapped it like a rug to get the sand off, but she took it from him before he could do it again and slid it on over her head, wet sand and all.

Fisher watched her struggle with her dress and wanted to help her, but some instinct told him to let her do it. He found his own clothes in a tangled wad on the sand and separated them out and pulled them on. He felt very strange and he didn't know quite how to act. He could still feel her against him like the ghost of a sensation. He could smell her even now; like she said, green, oddly fragrant. The smell of the water. It hardly seemed real. *She* hardly seemed real, hardly a girl at all, something less substantial.

"I guess we should go back," he said, because it was all he could think of to say.

Donna crossed her arms over her chest in a way that made her look very lonely. She looked at him from under her brows. Then quite suddenly she uncrossed them and offered him her hand, crooked awkwardly down at the wrist.

"Why don't you hold my hand," she said, her voice very soft. She sounded like she might cry.

And so he held her hand. It was cold and gritty with sand and he held it tight and led her back along the dark path toward the brightly lit gazebo where the dance was still going on, cautious couples going round and round to a slow song, barely touching, the careful elders unmoving in their lawn chairs stolid as eastern idols, watching over them all. Fisher could feel a halo of guilt white and ghostly as the river spring out from his skin. It glowed over them both, hot in the gray moonlight, and Fisher wondered if it would be there like an annunciation for the rest of his life.

He saw the Pastor's wife sitting with the other adults. She seemed relaxed there, her hair pulled back, her legs crossed carefully beneath her long skirt. She was smiling and talking and Fisher thought, *something—the stuff in the river or the smell of the water or God himself—has changed us all.*

He gripped Donna's cold hand and they walked into the wash of bright, clean light like the first lovers walking into the punishment that is the world.

ACKNOWLEDGMENTS

★

Grateful acknowledgment is made to the following publications in which some of these stories first appeared (some in earlier versions): *Berkeley Fiction Review* ("Swimming the Cave"); *Green Mountains Review* ("Trash Fish"); and *Shenandoah* ("Happy Puppy").

I would like to thank Mike Orloff of Martindale Motorcycle Works for sharing his mechanical expertise. I would also like to thank John Ledbetter, Dave Orloff, Tammy James, and my father, Ronald Blair, who all know why, or should.